Humleby Farm 3

Working Like
a Horse!

Malin Stehn

Working Like a Horse!

Copyright: Text copyright ©Malin Stehn 2009
Original title: Vilket hästjobb!
Cover and inside illustrations: © 2009 Strika Entertainment (Pty) Ltd.
Cape Town, South Africa
Cover layout: Stabenfeldt AS

Translated by Kjell Johansson
Typeset by Roberta L. Melzl
Editor: Bobbie Chase
Printed in Germany, 2009

ISBN: 978-1-934983-31-7

Stabenfeldt, Inc.
225 Park Avenue South
New York, NY 10003
www.pony4kids.com

Available exclusively through PONY.

For everybody who thinks animals are the greatest!

The New Girl in Class

"Hurry up, Mom! I'll be late!" Sofie could feel anxiety and irritation spreading through her body. "I totally refuse to be late on the first day!"

"I'm coming, I'm coming!" she heard Elizabeth's voice from the second floor. "I just don't know where I put the car keys. They're always in the side pocket …" A soft thud and the sound of coins rolling across the wooden floor told Sofie that her mom had just dropped her purse.

Sofie nervously looked at the kitchen clock, whose second hand relentlessly moved around the dial. She stomped the floor in frustration.

It was so typical! Why did the car keys have to disappear this very morning? Of all the mornings in the history of the world, this was the worst. Sofie thought that this had to mean that God or the universe was on her case. There could be no other reason why she had to be late today.

"I found them!" Elizabeth suddenly came running down the stairs. She had her open purse in one hand and dangled the car keys triumphantly in the other. "I'd put them in the inner compartment," she happily explained, slipping her feet into a pair of black ballerina slippers. "New purses are hopeless, don't you think?"

5

"Let's go," Sofie said tightly, not answering her question. "We have exactly seven minutes."

Elizabeth straightened her skirt and looked in the mirror on the wall.

"You've got everything?" she asked.

"I have my backpack. What else could I need?" Sofie was already outside. "Mom, *please,*" she asked, "just hurry up!"

Elizabeth walked out the door, carefully closed it behind her and locked it. She drew a breath of fresh morning air through her nose and sighed in satisfaction.

This would be a lovely late summer day. The sun shone from a clear blue sky as the fragrant smell of ripe apples and roses swept by. The pink geraniums on the brick wall were blooming for the second or third time this season and were bursting with pink petals. Elizabeth loved August.

"Oh!" she exclaimed. "What a lovely day!"

A *lovely* day? Sofie was close to falling apart.

"Mom…" she slowly growled through her teeth. Her jaw was so tight it hurt.

"You'll be on time!" Elizabeth gave her daughter an encouraging smile and opened the gate to the garage driveway where one of the family's cars was parked. Sofie jumped into the passenger seat.

"We'll see," she muttered.

If it had been an ordinary day, Sofie would have looked for Lisa and Mrs. Brown, the two brown warm-blooded mares that roamed the paddock next to the driveway. She would probably also have noticed that George, the horses' owner, was waving to her from the stable yard on the other side of the street.

But instead of looking out the car window, Sofie stared at the digital clock on the dashboard.

6

It was now 8:10. This meant that she had exactly five minutes to get to class. In five minutes, she should be standing in front of a crowd of strange faces and being introduced as "the new girl."

She already knew exactly how it would go. Everybody would stare at her. They would measure her with their eyes, from head to toes. Some of them would whisper together, just to make her uncertain. A few others would look at her with superior smiles, while most would pretend to be uninterested.

She knew all this from experience, since it's always the same when a new person joins a group where everybody already knows each other.

Not that Sofie had been the new person very often, but she had been sitting in the big confident group many times, while new classmates were introduced to her.

At those times, she hadn't thought about how terrible it must be for those girls and boys who were squirming in front of the class. She hadn't known why their eyes were shifty and why they looked so worried and unsure. Now, she understood perfectly.

Just a couple of months ago, Sofie and her family had moved back to Sweden after ten years in London. Stefan, Sofie's dad, was a doctor and had received a new job offer at the hospital in the city, in downtown Malmö. In spite of this, Sofie's parents had chosen to move to a place more than five miles out of town. This meant that after living most of her life in one of the biggest cities of the world, Sofie now lived in Humleby, a village with thirteen houses and two stables – and where most of the villagers were horses, not people.

During the first weeks, Sofie had hated living in the country. Actually, she had hated the whole idea of moving back to Sweden.

Leaving her best friend Jojo had been worst of all, but saying goodbye to the big city had also been sad. Sofie only had a few memories from her first three years in Sweden. London, with their semi-detached house in Barnes, was Sofie's real childhood home. And she'd had to leave it very quickly.

During the summer, Sofie had worked for her uncle and aunt, who owned a big trotting stable in the center of the village. She had slowly learned to appreciate both country life and her job as a horse-minder. Sofie had spent most of her time with her fifteen-year-old cousin Isabelle and had actually hardly met a soul who either didn't work at the stable or wasn't related to her.

Sofie's big sister Emma had spent her summer vacation in Humleby, but about a week ago she'd gone back to London to continue her college studies. Jojo had also been over for a visit, but she, too, was back in England.

The grim truth was that Sofie knew nobody in her class. And since Humleby was so out of the way, she knew none of the teenagers in the area. A few times, when she and Isabelle had ridden their bikes down to the gas station to buy ice cream, she had seen a few girls her own age, but she hoped they weren't in her class. They looked snobbish and stuck up.

"There!" Elizabeth said, pulling up in front of the school. "Have a nice day, honey!" She patted Sofie's cheek. "You remember where you're supposed to go?"

Sofie nodded and jumped out of the car. She felt that if she tried to say anything she'd start to cry, and she certainly didn't want to look red-eyed when she got gawked at by a roomful of strangers.

"I'll pick you up at three!" Elizabeth called through the open car window. But Sofie didn't answer. She had already run halfway across the schoolyard, tightly gripping her backpack in one hand.

❀ ❀ ❀ ❀

At the very second that the last school bell died out, Sofie stepped across the threshold of the classroom where she had been summoned by letter a couple of weeks ago. She was glad that the teacher hadn't made it there before her. The mood in the room was chaotic and nobody seemed to notice the new girl, who sat down quietly in a chair at the back of the room.

Everybody talked at the same time. An eraser flew through the air and hit a boy in the forehead. Somebody laughed.

Three girls stood in the middle of the room, studying a cell phone display. They were talking loudly to attract the interest of some boys who were standing next to them. But as soon as the boys went over to look, they were pushed away as the girls erupted in fits of violent giggles.

Sofie knew this game. It was just like being back with her old classmates at the Swedish School in London. The only difference was that she didn't know anybody here. The people who owned these faces were strangers.

"Good morning!" A powerful voice made the group quiet down a little and everybody looked toward the door.

A fit, tanned man in his forties, maybe a little younger, decisively stepped up to the teacher's desk and put down two big stacks of paper. Then he stood at the blackboard, waiting.

After a minute of chair scraping and general confusion, everybody found a place to sit, and then it was more or less quiet.

"Good morning," the man said again.

"Good morning," most of the students answered.

"Welcome back to school. I guess you've been looking

forward to this day all summer long!" Scattered groans were heard around the classroom. The tanned man smiled broadly, revealing a set of even, very white teeth. "No, but seriously," he said, standing up. "My name is Jimmy, and I'll be your homeroom teacher for the next three years. I recognize most of you. I guess many of you know that I'm a Phys Ed teacher here at school – I'm sure we've met in the corridors or in the lunch room." Jimmy looked at the class. "But I see there are a few new faces… At least one!" His eyes locked on Sofie.

So this was it. Sofie dearly wished she could sink through the floor and disappear forever, but in spite of all her prayers nothing happened. She sat on her uncomfortable chair as twenty-five pairs of curious eyes stared at her.

Sofie broke out in a cold sweat. She hoped that her hair wasn't too messy after her run across the schoolyard. She knew that her clothes were all right, or at least she had felt that way when she chose them yesterday.

Suddenly, she wasn't sure of her clothes at all. When she looked around, she thought that all the other girls looked very trendy. Several wore miniskirts, a few were made up and many had long, dangling earrings.

Sofie had had a discussion with herself and decided that she didn't want to be too visible. Being new in class was quite enough to get people's attention, and she certainly didn't want people to think she was bigheaded just because she had lived in London.

That was why she was now sitting in the back of the classroom, dressed in a pair of blue jeans and feeling like a space alien. Jeans and hoodies were Sofie's favorite clothes, but right now she wished that she had dressed a little more trendily.

Jimmy took a paper from one of the stacks on his desk and then looked at Sofie again.

"You're Sofie, right?"

Sofie nodded. She still felt as if she would cry if she tried to speak.

"Great!" Jimmy smiled. "Sofie Lindquist is new in class and I hope you'll take good care of her. Do you want to say anything about yourself?"

Sofie shook her head.

"Okay." Jimmy smiled again. "We'll do that another day. Are there any volunteers to show Sofie around the school and make her feel at home here?"

The room was so quiet that one could have heard an eraser fall on the gray linoleum floor.

"No?" Jimmy took a paper from the desk, looked at it for a moment and then said, "Nathalie Almgren. Which one of you is Nathalie?"

A blonde girl on the other side of the room unwillingly raised her hand. Judging from her expression, she wasn't too happy with her task. Jimmy, on the other hand, looked very happy.

"Nathalie," he said, firing off another dazzling smile, "it's your task to take care of Sofie. And I trust you to do a good job."

"Sure," the girl named Nathalie said, without looking in Sofie's direction.

"Great. It's a deal then! And of course, you can come see me anytime, too," Jimmy said, looking at Sofie again.

Sofie nodded silently.

Jimmy took a roll call, from Nathalie Almgren to Tom Zetterberg, and noted everybody with a pen. Then he took one stack of paper and started handing out sheets to everybody.

12

"This is a makeshift class list," he explained. "You'll get a more complete school directory in about a month… Which reminds me that you'll be photographed soon. I'll check the times in a minute."

Jimmy kept on handing out the sheets as he spoke energetically.

"At the bottom of your class lists you'll find my phone number and my e-mail address if you need them. Don't hesitate to contact me. If you're sick, report to the main office before eight a.m."

During the following twenty minutes, the class was totally assaulted with information about the coming year. Sofie felt as if her brain were swelling inside her skull.

By the time the bell rang, she was weak in the knees. Names of teachers and numbers of classrooms were spinning around in her head, and she was sure she had missed half of everything Jimmy had said. The last thing he called after his students when they left the room was, "Don't forget your photo session tomorrow morning! Eight fifteen sharp – in the library!"

Sofie hated having her picture taken. School photos were the worst kind, since you knew the entire school would be sitting at home laughing at you if the photo didn't turn out well. And just because you didn't want to make a funny face, you always *made* a funny face.

Sofie remembered her class photo from fifth grade. Jojo had managed to tickle her right when the camera flashed. The result was a Sofie with flailing arms and tightly closed eyes.

"Are you coming?" Sofie was shaken out of her daydream by Nathalie, who was leaning against the wall outside the classroom with two other girls.

Sofie hurried and followed her classmates, who quickly

13

started walking toward the glass doors of the staircase. She felt like a dog out for a walk with a quick-stepping master.

Nathalie and the two other girls spoke animatedly to each other, not bothering to let their new classmate in on the conversation. Sofie thought that they looked a lot older than she, closer to Isabelle's age. She couldn't quite pinpoint why. Maybe it was their clothes and hair – or maybe it was just that she felt so small and unsure of herself.

There was also something about Nathalie that seemed familiar, but since Sofie was sure she didn't know any girl her age in this town, that was impossible.

It wasn't until they were sitting in the auditorium listening to the headmaster's welcome speech that Sofie realized it was Nathalie and her friends she had seen at the gas station over the summer vacation. She sighed at her bad luck. Those uptight girls at the gas station could have been at any school, she thought bitterly. But destiny obviously had other plans.

Sofie couldn't fathom how she would be able to spend most of her time in this terrible school, with all these unfriendly, snobbish kids. She hated her parents for making her move from London, and especially from Jojo and the Swedish School. She felt as if she would do almost anything to turn the clock back a few months and change everything.

If it had been possible – if she had been able to wake up and have it be March again – no doubt she would have put all her energy into erasing her dad's job offer from the face of the earth. She would have thrown away all letters with his name on them, watched the phone, thrown his cell phone into the Thames River and hid his computer in some clever place.

It didn't matter that she would have lost Isabelle's friendship and that she never would have gotten to know Tina and the others at Humleby Farm. She could live without them.

And when Sofie, from the corner of her eye, watched Nathalie and her friends whispering with their heads close, she almost felt that she could live without Speedy Legend and all the wonderful horses in the village. If she could just go back to her old school again.

More Bad News

"Hi, honey! How was your day?" Elizabeth smiled at her daughter, who thumped into the passenger seat.

"Horrible," Sofie said, slamming the door shut. She stared out at the parking lot without meeting her mother's eyes.

"B-but…" Elizabeth didn't really know how to handle this. From experience, she knew that Sofie could be something of a drama queen sometimes – in other words, she could exaggerate things a little. All the same, she didn't want to ignore her daughter's comment and forget about the whole thing. Sofie really *could* have had a horrible day.

"Do you want to tell me about it?" she asked softly, putting her hand on top of Sofie's.

"No." Sofie pulled her hand away and clenched her jaw.

She really wanted to scream. She wanted to yell that all this was Elizabeth's fault, that it was her mom – and dad Stefan – who had decided that the family had to move, and that because of this it was *their* fault that her life was ruined forever.

But Sofie knew that her mother would just sing her old song about Stefan's new job being impossible to turn down, that they wanted to live closer to Sofie's aging grandparents and that everything would work out in the end.

16

The part about "everything working out" was the last thing Sofie wanted to hear right now. Yes, it was true that this was exactly what Elizabeth had said after Sofie's first day as a horse minder at Humleby Farm. And that time it actually *had* worked out. Sofie had stopped being scared to death of horses. She had even started liking them – and she had also become good friends with Isabelle, something that had seemed completely impossible at first.

But this time Sofie was sure that there was no happy ending. Everybody in her class, all the girls and boys, seemed self-absorbed and stuck up. Nobody had said a single word to her the whole day – except Nathalie, who had been forced to.

It was true that Sofie felt thankful to Jimmy for not cross-examining her in front of the class, but at the same time she thought it was weird that he didn't keep her for a while after the first class. The least he could have done was ask if everything was okay and if she had any questions.

Nobody had asked her where she was from or what school she had gone to. And Sofie had actually wanted to tell the class a little about London, their semi-detached house in Barnes, the Swedish School and Jojo. Then, at least, she would have been Sofie from London.

Right now it felt like she was Sofie from the country of Nowhere, without a past – and without a future.

"Did you get the school bus schedule?" Elizabeth turned into the driveway of their house, parked the car and took the keys.

"Yes."

"That's good. So let's check out the times."

Sofie didn't answer. Just the thought of sitting on the same bus as a lot of weird little kids and stuck-up students her own age every morning and afternoon made her sick.

"You might as well try riding it tomorrow, so we'll

know how it works. I start my job on Monday," Elizabeth reminded her daughter.

"I know."

Sofie didn't want to think about Elizabeth starting work. Sofie's mom hadn't had a real job since Sofie was born – but on the other hand, she had been busy with various associations and charity projects during all their years in England. Sofie was worried that it would be a huge change for the family not to have Elizabeth at home any more. Sofie and her dad were both spoiled by not having to do many household chores. For as long as Sofie could remember, there had always been clean, well-ironed clothes in her closet. The house had always been tidy, and there had almost always been food on the table every evening at five thirty.

Sofie's mom never complained. She liked cooking and taking care of the house. But Emma had left home long ago and Sofie was now in seventh grade. This would mean longer days in school, and Elizabeth was afraid that she would get bored just being at home.

By coincidence, she had heard of a job opening, teaching English in evening courses. She had applied for the job, gotten it, and announced to the family that from now on things would change. Sofie suspected that this meant everybody would have to help out with food preparation, cleaning and so on.

"Want a bun?" Elizabeth asked, as if she had heard Sofie's thoughts. "I have a few in the freezer."

"No thanks." Sofie threw her backpack on the floor and made a U-turn. "I'm going to the stable."

"Okay." Elizabeth couldn't really hide her disappointment. She had been looking forward to having a cup of coffee and hearing what Sofie had to say about her first day at school, but she also knew that trying to persuade her daughter to stay

18

home was useless. She looked out the window as Sofie left the driveway and turned onto the village road. Watching the miserable figure walk toward Humleby Farm with heavy steps and hanging head, Elizabeth hoped with all her heart that Isabelle would be home from school soon. Maybe Sofie would open up to her?

❀ ❀ ❀ ❀

"Hi, Sofie!"

"What's up?"

"Hello!"

Sofie was met by lots of cheery calls and smiles as she crossed the yard in front of Humleby Farm's red buildings. This felt nice after having been treated like dirt for most of the day.

Because of this, Sofie managed to meet her former fellow workers with a smile, despite her sullen mood. Well, actually, they were still her fellow workers, but only on weekends. When her summer job at Humleby Farm had ended, her uncle – in a move that made her very happy – had asked her if she would like to help out in the stable on Saturdays and Sundays.

Sofie hadn't hesitated for a moment. First of all, she loved working in the stable and being with the wonderful trotting horses there. And second, she didn't have much else to do. Isabelle was the only girl she knew in the entire town roughly her age – and Isabelle always helped her parents on the weekends.

Elizabeth and Stefan weren't too fond of the idea of having her work every weekend.

"You have to do your homework," Stefan had said. "You'll have more of it now."

"I can do that in the afternoons, after school," Sofie had answered quickly.

Elizabeth had joined in, "But you're bound to make a

lot of new friends whom you'll want to see. And you might want to try some other activity – like soccer or…"

"Did I ever say I wanted to play soccer?" Sofie had quickly retorted.

"It was just an example," Elizabeth tried to explain.

The discussion had ended there, and the next day Sofie had accepted the job offer. She knew that her parents were partly right. There would be more homework in seventh grade than before, no doubt about that. But they could forget that stuff about friends and other activities. Sofie figured that it was quite enough to use the weekdays for school and homework. Then she would be able to spend the weekends on her favorite pastime; taking care of the horses at Humleby Farm. This was going to be her reward for studying hard all week.

Sofie went into the little stable, one of the four stables at the farm and the one that had been her principal workplace all summer. She inhaled the cozy smell of horses and hay and relaxed a little.

Strangely, the stable – a place that Sofie had hated vehemently when the summer began – had become kind of her home away from home. She loved being in the little stable. Sometimes she went there in the evenings, when the other horse minders had gone home, just to be alone with the horses and enjoy the friendly silence.

It was at these moments that Sofie felt she could really be herself. She could talk about how much she missed Jojo, about wanting to trade places with her big sister, or about how she hated starting a new class at a new school.

The horses seemed to listen. They pricked their ears forward and looked at her with their dark, wise eyes. And they never protested, never seemed to worry on her behalf, and never asked troublesome questions.

Sofie went straight to the box in the inner right corner to say hello to her personal favorite, Speedy Legend. Speedy was a famous trotter that had won the derby[1] a year ago, but had then been injured and ended up with an owner who didn't care about him.

Now, Speedy was owned by an elderly man named Axel. Axel had contacted Sofie's uncle, one of the best trotting trainers in Sweden, and Speedy had arrived at the Sandberg family's Humleby Farm just as Sofie started her summer job there.

Now Speedy Legend was back at the racetrack. Just a few days ago, the chestnut gelding had won a race at Jägersro, the local track for Humleby Farm. It was a great victory.

Sofie couldn't really say why she had fallen immediately for the beautiful chestnut. Maybe it was because the two of them had been new to the stable at the same time – or it could simply be that he was an unusually beautiful horse.

To Sofie, it felt as if she had met her second twin soul. (Jojo was her first.) Of course, Speedy wasn't very talkative – but when she met his eyes, she somehow always found comfort. She often felt that he could read her thoughts and that he understood her better than any other living being.

"Hi, boy!" Sofie reached out toward the gelding's muzzle with her hand. "Are you waiting to be let out in the paddock?"

Speedy always went outside at night. He shared a paddock with Sky, a dark brown gelding. About half of the horses at Humleby were "outsiders," while the other half slept in the stables.

This was partly due to the fact that there weren't enough

---

1 The Swedish Trotting Derby is an annual highly prestigious race for 4-year old horses, held at Jägersro trav och galopp (trotting and galloping track) in Malmö, Sweden.

paddocks for all the horses – about forty of them – that Sofie's uncle Tommy was training. But it also had to do with the fact that some of the four-legged tenants were fidgety and felt better inside. All the "insiders" went out in the paddocks for most of the day anyway, which meant that every horse in the stable got to stretch his or her legs outside every day.

It was almost three thirty and Sofie knew Tina would be showing up any time now to take Speedy and Sky out to their paddock. Two of the inside horses, Tornado and Rocky, were already in place, back in their freshly mucked-out boxes.

Speedy bent forwards and sniffed Sofie's hand. Then he let out some air through his big nostrils and nudged her lightly.

"I forgot to bring treats," Sofie said, caressing the gelding's white blaze. "I'm sorry, I was only thinking of myself today."

Speedy snorted, and Sofie couldn't really decide if he was upset or if he meant that it was okay for this one time.

"I promise to bring some apples next time," she assured him.

Sofie had hardly been able to get near to a horse when she arrived at Humleby two months earlier. She had thought that the big animals were terrifying!

Now, however, she wasn't scared of horses anymore, but she still felt great respect for Speedy and his friends. She had a lot to learn.

She still had never taken care of any of the stallions, since they were too unpredictable. But after two months in the stable Sofie could put on head collars and bridles, and groom and lead horses to and from their paddocks. She showered them after their training runs and was starting to get the hang of how to wrap their legs.

Sofie also hadn't tried driving yet. Humleby Farm was a trotting stable, and of course horses were mostly driven with a long wagon[2] or a sulky. That was an activity Sofie wasn't very eager to learn, at least yet.

On the other hand, she had been thinking about riding one of the horses. Jenny, one of the horse-minders, had actually promised to help her do that.

Jenny worked in the upper stable, but she saw to it that most of Humleby Farm's horses were ridden now and then. This gave the trotters a workout of other muscle groups than the ones used for driving.

Sofie's biggest dream was to ride Speedy Legend – she thought it would be a great way to get even closer to him.

Once in a while, she imagined herself riding the gelding chestnut, flying across the fields in a wild gallop. But not even Jenny had tried riding him yet, so Sofie knew that her dream would stay a dream for quite some time.

Speedy had been very nervous and troubled when he came to the farm. He had calmed down in just a few days, but Tommy had wanted to concentrate on just driving the horse.

Now that Speedy had won his first race in over a year, Sofie hoped that the gelding would be ready for some all-around exercise, which could include Jenny starting to ride him. And maybe Sofie would be next.

Of course, it would be smart for her to try another horse first, Sofie mused as she slowly stroked Speedy's nose. The chestnut stood very still, eyes half closed, obviously enjoying the attention.

"Hi, Sofie! Good to see you!"

Tina's voice made Sofie jump. She turned around and saw the shorthaired woman in the stable door.

2 In training trotters, a long wagon is always used. The driver sits better in a long wagon than in a sulky, which is used during races. The long wagon is also safer, since the driver sits further away from the horse.

"Hi!" she said.

Tina, who was a small but muscular woman in her thirties, walked into the passageway. She was bringing Champion and Oh My Glory, two beautiful geldings, with her, and she quickly tied them both in the passageway.

Tina was one of the oldest minders at Humleby Farm, and she had been the one to teach Sofie her job that summer.

Sofie liked Tina. She was kind, a true animal lover and genuinely interested in her job. Also, she was dependable. Tina never jumped to conclusions, and Sofie had never heard her talking about people behind their backs.

"So, how was school today?" The blonde horse-minder picked up her grooming kit and walked over to Champion, who was first in line to be groomed.

"Don't want to talk about it." Sofie had managed to forget her troubles for a while, and Tina's words threw her right back into grim reality.

Tina frowned.

"That bad?" Her brown eyes looked into Sofie's blue ones.

Sofie nodded.

"I wish I didn't have to go back…" The tears were close now. Sofie looked down at the ground to avoid Tina's compassionate look.

Tina checked her work on Champion's coat. She straightened, walked up to Sofie and put a comforting hand on her shoulder.

"Today was just the first day," she said calmly. "Don't you remember how terrible you thought your first day at Humleby Farm was?"

"Yes…" Sofie nodded again.

"It'll get better. I know it can be terrible to go to a new class and a new school, but you can manage it. You managed your summer job here, didn't you?"

Sofie looked up and smiled weakly at the blonde woman. "Yes, yeah…"

Tina let go of Sofie's shoulder and went back to Champion, who seemed confused by the sudden interruption. He tried in vain to turn around to see what was going on.

"I'm sure you'll like school better in just a week," Tina said and patted Champion's neck to soothe him. "By then, you'll know your way around and know everybody by name."

"Well, maybe," Sofie said slowly. But deep inside, she didn't believe Tina even for a moment. Sofie didn't think she would ever be able to like that school.

"I'm sorry, but I don't have any good news to perk you up." Tina looked sadly at Sofie over her shoulder.

"What?" Sofie felt worry creeping up on her. "Has something happened?"

"Yes, actually it's Speedy…" Tina looked at her again. "Something is wrong."

Get Me Out of Here!

"B-but…" Sofie looked at Tina in horror. "He *won* last Tuesday! And he was completely fine yesterday!"

The blonde woman nodded.

"There's something wrong with the knee on his right foreleg. I noticed him limping this morning when I took him in. It might be that he's overworked. The knee seems a little swollen…"

Sofie went up to the box and peered in through the bars. She clearly saw which knee was hurting Speedy. How had she missed it?

"Oh!" she said. "What happens now?"

"Andersson will be here tomorrow. We'll just have to hope for the best," Tina said. Andersson was the vet that Humleby Farm used.

"And if it turns out to be serious?" Sofie couldn't keep herself from asking, although she already knew what Tina's answer would be.

"No use worrying about that until we know more."

Sofie sighed. If she ever wished that Tina would make more guesses, it was when it came to Speedy. She would have felt a lot better if Tina made a few reassuring remarks. At least, it would have been momentarily comforting.

"Has his knee ever bothered him before?" Sofie watched the chestnut, who had turned around to taste the hay on the floor beneath his feeder.

"I don't think so…" Tina thought for a while. "His injury after the derby was in one hock."

"Will he have to stay inside tonight?" Sofie asked. She knew that Speedy loved being outside and that he got the jitters if he had to be in his box for too long.

"Yes, I think it's best to keep him still until we know why he's lame."

Sofie stood by Speedy's box for a long time. Usually, she would have asked Tina if there was anything she could do, but the news about her favorite horse's health had made what little energy she had left disappear into thin air. It felt like her legs were cast in lead, and her brain seemed to be swimming around in molasses or some other viscous liquid.

When Tina was done grooming Champion and Oh My Glory, she turned to Sofie. "Would you like to come along and let the ladies out in their paddock?"

She unhooked two lead reins from the wall.

The "ladies" were the two mares in the little stable, Divine Star and Leading Lady. They used the paddock right next to the one where Sky and Speedy used to be.

"Love to," Sofie said, reaching out to grab one lead rein. She hoped that the walk might be able to push her dark thoughts away.

"Now don't worry too much about Speedy," Tina said. "It doesn't *have to* be serious just because his knee is swollen. He's probably just overworked, which means he'll just need a shot."

Sofie opened the door to Lady's box.

"Okay," she said, stepping onto the soft sawdust. "I'll try to think of it that way."

"Actually, I wasn't going to tell you about Speedy's knee until I knew more about it." Tina's voice came from Star's box. "Now I'm afraid I've totally ruined your day."

"It's not your fault that Speedy's lame." Sofie pushed her forearm against Lady's shoulder to make her turn in the right direction. Then she snapped the lead rein onto the bridle and led the brown mare out of the box.

Tina and Star were waiting in the yard. Tina squinted in the sharp sunlight.

"I know it's not my fault that Speedy's lame." She smiled and pulled down her cap to shadow her eyes. "It's just that I had a feeling your first day at school would be taxing, and after a horrible day like that, you didn't come here to hear about a lot of problems."

"Horrible day is right." Sofie couldn't help smiling back at Tina. She couldn't have said it better herself.

It had been a horrible day.

They started walking toward the furthest paddocks. Tina and Star went first, Sofie and Lady right behind them. When they turned into the little gravel road that wormed through the foliage, Tina turned around.

"Come to think of it…" she said. "When things are at their worst, they can only get better, right?"

Sofie nodded, but she wasn't sure Tina was right. She didn't doubt that Speedy would get well – but at school, things could certainly get worse. A whole lot worse.

❁ ❁ ❁ ❁

By the time they got back to the stables, Tina's workday was over. Sofie went in to see Speedy again, but he seemed asleep, so she decided to look for Isabelle instead.

Sofie walked around the big stable and then toward the Sandberg's house, which was on the edge of the grounds, in a leafy yard with lots of old gnarled fruit trees. Right now the trees were weighted down with apples, pears and plums, all smelling sweet.

The front door was open, but nobody answered when Sofie called, and she gave up after her third try. Out in the yard she met Maggie, Isabelle's mom, walking toward her briskly with the day's mail under her arm.

Maggie was as engaged in the family business as her husband; they owned the farm together. Tommy planned the training for the different horses and took care of most of the paperwork, while Maggie was more visible out in the stables. She was the boss in the stables and made sure everything went according to plan. Still, she wasn't the type to go around checking up on her personnel. She gave a helping hand where it was needed, and even had a few horses of her own to take care of. Maggie seldom stood still for more than a minute.

"Hi, Sofie!" she called cheerily. "How are you?"

"Fine." Sofie couldn't bear talking any more about school, so she quickly asked, "Is Isabelle here?"

"No." Maggie threw a quick glance at her watch. "She got off to a flying start with classes that lasted all the way till three thirty today. Then I think she and Marie planned to go to town to buy clothes…"

"Okay. I might call her later."

"You do that." Maggie hurried on and Sofie slowly walked in the opposite direction. She felt a little jealous when she thought about Isabelle. Her more than two years older cousin had also started at a new school in a new class today – but in that class, everybody was new, and also Isabelle had her best friend Marie with her. They were in their first year at the Natural Resource High School, in a program specializing in horses and horse-tending. A substantial part of the education would be hands-on training

30

at a learning stable at Jägersro, where the students got to learn almost everything about taking care of horses in a professional way – and they would get practical experience at other stables, too.

"Don't you know all that stuff already?" Sofie had said to her cousin as they were talking about the program.

"Well, I guess I know the practical stuff, but it's going to be fun to learn the theory. And I'll just have to try to stand English and math." Isabelle made a face.

"But don't you think it's going to be boring?" Sofie had pressed on.

"Nothing about horses can ever be boring!" Isabelle had answered, and then continued, "And even if I already know most of the stuff, it's not enough. I have to have some *proof* of what I know. That is to say, grades."

Sofie knew that Isabelle's dream was to be a professional trotting driver. She was already good at it – and since she had more or less grown up in a trotting stable, it was easy to understand why.

Sofie wished she were as old as Isabelle. Then maybe she would have been in the same class with her cousin. Whether or not she actually wanted to attend the Natural Resources program was besides the point – at least that way she would have had a friend in her class.

From: Sofie Lindquist <sofiesofine@swede-mail.com>
Date: Thursday, August 22, 2009, 17:16
To: Joanna Nilsson <jojo_sweetie@britmail.com>
Subject: Get me out of here!

Hi Jojo!
How was your first day in school? (I think you started today, too?)

My day was horrible. I'll just say one thing: Be happy that you're still in London! Remember that every time you feel whiny, because I can guarantee that whatever the problem is, you're still better off than I am.

My class teacher looks like Ken. (You know, of Barbie and Ken.) He actually seems kind of okay, but he was totally in a rush and just said, "hi" to me.

Everybody in class would fit in a fashion magazine, and one of the biggest snobs has been appointed to take care of me. Her name is Nathalie and I know she's only doing it because Ken told her to.

Nathalie and her two friends, Fanny and Camilla, dragged me around all day, but they didn't say one word to me. They just giggled and whispered to each other the whole time.

Would the two of us have been such creeps if a new girl had come to our class?

As if all this isn't bad enough, Speedy is hurt. I don't know how bad it is – Tina seems pretty calm, but I can't help worrying.

Do I sound pessimistic and boring? In that case, you're dead on. I don't think I'll ever be happy again.

Why do we have to go to school? If I had just been able to work at Humleby Farm instead of getting moldy on a school bench, life would have been perfect. I was just starting to like it here, but now everything just feels terrible.

Come and get me out of here!

Hugs,
Sofie

P.S. Was your trip home all right?

From: Joanna Nilsson <jojo_sweetie@britmail.com>
Date: Thursday, August 22, 2009, 18:30
To: Joanna Nilsson <sofiesofine@swede-mail.com>
Subject: Re: Get me out of here!

Hi, Sofa!

Nice to hear from you, even if the things you're writing about don't sound too fun.

I know it must be just terribly embarrassing to be new in class. I'm happy I don't have to do that. But I'm sure things will be better as soon as you get to know your classmates. There has to be at least <u>one</u> of the girls in your class who isn't <u>totally</u> brain dead. (I'm not saying you have to become best friends – after all, you've got me! :-) – but you really should be able to talk to a few of them during breaks and so on. Don't you think?)

I'm sure Speedy will get well soon. Not that I'm a horse expert, but he seemed to be in really great shape last Tuesday.

You know what? You're going to go crazy now, but I have to tell the truth: Actually, I'm almost a little jealous of you!

Well, not that I long to meet that Nathalie or anything like that – but at least something is <u>happening</u> in your life. My life is at a complete standstill. I live in the same old house, go to the same old school and in the same old class… The only thing that has happened is that you moved away, and because of that, none of the rest of this is any fun.

You do have your weekend job at the stable and a whole school full of new, exciting people to get to know! (Maybe there even are a few good-looking boys to flirt with?)

Never mind Nathalie and her silly buddies. Find the cool people – you have every opportunity.

I spoke a little with Jessica today. She seemed to regret what she wrote to me over the summer, but I'm not sure I can trust her anymore. I think I'll try to stay away from her as much as I can.

Miss you a lot! Hope we can meet during fall break!

Hugs,
Jojo

P.S. My trip home was fine. I was sitting pressed between two horribly huge businessmen on the plane and could hardly move – but I did get home at last!

The Queen of the Class

"Bye! Have a nice day!"

Elizabeth stood in the door waving to Sofie, who had just disappeared around the corner. The neighbor's wife had told them that the school bus stopped right next to their mailbox. Their oldest son was in the first grade at Sofie's school and he took the bus.

Sofie clenched her teeth. A nice day? How could her mother stand there and wish her "a nice day," when she was headed for a torture chamber obviously specializing in slow, painful deaths?

There was nothing, absolutely nothing at all, to indicate that this would be one of the better days in Sofie's life. She just might be able to survive it, since it was Friday. As soon as she had made it through the first seven hours of Friday, she actually wouldn't have to see the disgusting school for two whole days.

Elizabeth and Stefan had tried nonstop to get their daughter to tell them a little about her first day at school. On Thursday night, they had used every conceivable trick to make Sofie talk; they had prodded, joked, begged and nagged.

But Sofie had been as silent as a wall. She knew that

whatever she said, it would be met with, "it's going to work out fine" and a pat on the head. Parents never took real problems seriously. On the other hand, they liked to blow up small problems.

Sofie had mechanically chewed the fish au gratin and gotten up from the table without saying a word. Then she had lain on her bed, crying in her pillow until she fell asleep.

When Stefan woke Sofie on Friday morning, she had tried to look as pale as possible as she whispered, "I don't feel too well. I guess I'll have to stay home today."

She knew what a transparent lie it was. Her parents weren't idiots. Of course they understood – by the way she acted – how she felt about her new school.

"Oh?" Stefan put his palm on Sofie's forehead. "Well, there's no fever, anyway."

"B-but I… >Cough, cough<! My throat hurts real bad," Sofie sputtered.

"Open your mouth!" Stefan quickly looked into Sofie's open mouth. His diagnosis was simple: "There are no signs at all of throat infection."

The doctor had spoken, and Sofie had no choice but to get out of bed.

All morning, she had felt like the loneliest, most misunderstood person in the whole world. When even Jojo wrote things like, "I'm sure it will get better," who could she turn to for comfort and support?

❄ ❄ ❄ ❄

"Hi, Sofie! It's great that you and I are on the same bus!"

Jack, the neighbor's boy, suddenly stood beside her at the bus stop. He was dressed in blue shorts and blue sneakers, and on his back was a black backpack with a Spiderman design.

"Hi." Sofie tried not to act grumpy toward Jack. After all, it wasn't his fault that she'd had to change schools.

"Nice bag, right?" Jack proudly turned around to let Sofie look at his backpack. "It's brand new," he told her. "Last year, when I was in kindergarten, I had a Winnie the Pooh backpack. But you can't have that when you're in first grade, can you!" He laughed and revealed a great gap in his mouth where new front teeth would grow in time.

Jack kept babbling without interruption, which made Sofie happy to see a gray bus behind a stand of trees. The big vehicle slowly rolled along between the foliage near the paddocks, and the sunshine glaring off the shiny gray paint. The bus with its modern design looked out of place in the idyllic landscape. Sofie felt like a spaceship was coming to take her far, far away to another galaxy.

That would have been perfect.

"Hi there!" The bus driver was an elderly woman with her hair tied in a knot at her neck. She wore a dark blue coat and pants of the same color. "How nice, a new traveler!" she said, showing a lot of laugh lines around her kind eyes. "Welcome!"

"Thank you." Sofie hoped that the driver's welcome greeting hadn't echoed in the entire bus. Most of all, she wanted to sink down in a seat and be as invisible as possible.

"Come on, Sofie!" Jack called. "Come and sit with me!"

Nobody could avoid hearing the shrill voice of the seven-year-old. To minimize the risk of further eruptions, Sofie hurried over to Jack and squeezed into the window seat next to him. She avoided looking around her, scared of discovering that some other passenger on the bus was in her class. What would she do if that happened? Would she say hello? And if she did, would the person return her greeting?

Sofie didn't feel like talking to anybody – not even Jack, although he was just a sweet, harmless little seven-year-old. Because of this, she was grateful when he turned away from her and started talking to a boy his own age across the aisle. In a moment, the two boys were in a heated conversation about Spiderman, and Sofie relaxed a little.

After a couple of minutes, she dared raise her head to squint at the people around her. She noted that she had been lucky – nobody close to her was her own age. She seemed to have been mixed up with the first and second graders.

At the last stop before school, a group of older boys got on the bus. They talked loudly in cracked teenage voices, patted each other's backs and acted like teenage boys usually do.

Although Sofie wasn't too fond of teenage boys with sprouting mustaches, she couldn't help looking at them. And she especially couldn't help looking a little longer at one of them. He was a little shorter than the others, had blond, curly hair and was – yes, she had to admit to herself – kind of cute. Sofie wondered if he was in eighth or ninth grade.

When the bus stopped at school, chaos ensued. Sofie had never understood the idea of throwing yourself off the bus when it stopped. Everybody got off the bus anyway, sooner or later.

Jack had already forgotten his travel companion and squeezed out through the doors with his friend.

Sofie was the very last person to leave the bus. She wished she could sit there all day, that she and the nice driver could take a day trip to someplace fun. To the sea, or to Denmark…

"Bye for now!" said the woman behind the wheel when Sofie left the bus. "Have a nice day!"

Sofie thought she saw a glint of compassion in the driver's eyes.

❀ ❀ ❀ ❀

There really were no advantages at all to riding the school bus.

First of all, you had to travel with a lot of strangers. Sofie liked peace and quiet in the mornings, and the school bus was just the opposite of that.

Secondly, you got to school way too early. The bus let the students off as early as five to eight. That meant that there were twenty long minutes to wait before the bell rang. Twenty minutes that Sofie had to be all alone in the schoolyard.

She walked over and stood to the left of the building. The branches of a small Norway maple tree reached out like a tent above the asphalt. Sofie stood under the tree, hoping to blend into the foliage and be as invisible as possible.

The hardest thing about feeling lonely was not revealing one's feelings. Although Sofie felt more desolate than ever before, she made an effort to look cool and busy. She definitely didn't want any of the teachers that were roaming the yard to come up and ask how she was – and maybe force some other poor kid to "take care" of her.

Sofie took out her cell phone and pretended to read something on the display. She stood there for a long time, staring at the ugly logo of the phone company. Then she pressed a few buttons, more or less randomly.

"That's a nice phone."

Sofie jumped when somebody suddenly spoke to her. It was Nathalie. She was a few feet away with her constant companions, Fanny and Camilla.

The three girls wore almost identical clothes, and Sofie

39

thought they looked silly. She remembered a story that her mom used to read to her when she was little. The story of Peter No-Tail was about a cat who was teased because he didn't have a tail. The worst bully was named Mons, and he always had two stupid, but very loyal, cat friends with him, named Bill and Bull.

"Thank you." Sofie quickly put the phone back in her pocket.

"That must be expensive… It's the latest model, right?" Nathalie crossed her arms and smiled, without the smile really reaching her eyes.

"Well… I don't know," Sofie said truthfully. "Dad gave it to me a while ago."

Nathalie smiled her cold smile again.

"Well, some people live the good life. Your father is a doctor, right?"

Sofie nodded. She wondered how the blonde girl knew anything about her family, and she was on the verge of asking when the school bell rang. The first ring echoed across the yard. Sofie demonstratively turned and started walking toward the main entrance. She was relieved that she didn't have to say anything more right now.

Nathalie, Fanny and Camilla were a few steps behind her, and Sofie could hear Nathalie loudly saying, "Spoiled people are the worst!"

Sofie wanted to turn around and yell that she had no right to accuse her of anything. She knew *nothing* about her and her life! So Nathalie had somehow found out that Sofie's father was a doctor – what did that have to do with how she was brought up or what her life was like?

Instead of yelling, Sofie clenched her teeth and hurried into the school. The first class was math and she wasn't looking forward to it at all, but at least it was better to sit in a classroom, with a teacher who watched what was said and done, than to be taunted out in the yard.

After the photo session, which was over in ten minutes, Sofie quickly walked to her locker and took out her math book and her pencil box. Then she squeezed her backpack in with her other books, closed the door and locked up. She had memorized the number of the room and knew more or less in which direction to go, but she was still happy when she could follow a couple of the boys in her class going to the same place. She decided to forget about Nathalie "taking care of her" – and it certainly didn't seem as if Nathalie wanted to care for her, either. At least, her attack out in the yard didn't seem very caring.

Almost everybody in the class was standing in the hallway outside the room. Nathalie and her little group were already there. Sofie saw that they were talking to

41

some other girls in the class – and since they fell silent the second she appeared it was easy to figure out what, or rather *whom*, they had been talking about.

In the Swedish School, they had often talked about bullying. As early as pre-school, the children had been encouraged to decide what a good friend was like, and they had been told to help and care for each other.

All the way up to fourth grade, Sofie had thought that bullying actually didn't exist in the real world. She was in a good class where everybody worked together, and apart from some friendly bickering, there had never been any problems.

But in fourth grade, the cozy feeling had disappeared totally. Ten new students had started in the class – among others, a girl who many thought was very cool and who most people looked up to.

Suddenly some of Sofie's friends, who had been very nice up till then, had changed abruptly. They started screaming at the teachers and openly bullied some students in the class – just to be popular with the new girl.

Sofie had hated Charlotte, the "cool" girl, but she hadn't dared to say anything. Instead, she and Jojo had kept more to themselves. At the time, they had felt that this was a good solution to the problem, but now she suddenly realized that she and Jojo had somehow let the bullied girls down. They had snuck away instead of telling Charlotte that she was acting bad.

Sofie guessed that Nathalie was just like Charlotte; somebody the other girls looked up to – and, maybe, were just a little afraid of. She wondered if Fanny, Camilla and all the others around Nathalie really, deep down, felt that it was okay to badmouth somebody who was new in class. But she would probably never know. Everybody seemed to be at Nathalie's beck and call. She was the queen of the class.

Sofie had had a lump in her throat when she woke up that morning. Now, it felt as if the lump had swelled to the size of a tennis ball and would burst any second.

Of course, there was really nothing wrong with her *throat*. Coughing and clearing her throat at home had been one last desperate attempt at staying home. She had known very well, all along, that it would never work. No doctor in the world can look down the throat of a patient and see aching tears.

Sofie swallowed. She could feel her eyes filling with tears. She desperately tried to avoid blinking – since that would make the tears well up and everybody would be able to tell that she was crying. She didn't want to treat Nathalie to that spectacle.

Just then, the math teacher came steaming down the corridor. Sofie sighed with relief when everybody looked at the little man with the pointed beard and the briefcase. She quickly blinked and wiped under her eyes with one sleeve.

When she looked up, she saw the curly-haired guy from the school bus. He came hurrying along with a book under one arm and almost crashed into Nathalie who, without bothering to look, stepped right out in the corridor. To avoid the collision, the boy jumped to the side and almost walked into Sofie.

"S-sorry!" He seemed to jump when he didn't recognize Sofie's face, and he kept his eyes on her for a moment. Then he hurried on.

"No problem," Sofie almost whispered, following his curly hair with her eyes. She had looked straight into a pair of totally fantastic hazel eyes.

Adam

Hi! Are you coming to the stable after school? Much to tell! Ciao! Isabelle

Sofie was going home on the school bus when her phone beeped. She was glad to get a message from her cousin and quickly answered:

On my way home. How's

She erased the last word and instead wrote:

On my way home. Be right over! S

Sofie had almost asked how Speedy was, but changed her mind after thinking about it for a moment. She didn't want to learn about her favorite horse by text message, and she decided to save her questions until she was at Humleby Farm. With luck, Tina would still be there to explain what the vet had said.

The school day had continued as it had begun – that is, quite as horribly. Several times, Sofie felt a compelling urge to storm out of the building and keep running all the way back to Humleby.

44

But of course, she had stayed. She knew that there was something called compulsory school attendance – a law saying that all children between the ages of seven and fifteen must attend school. She was also quite sure that her parents would hit the roof if she played hooky.

In English class, the young female teacher, just as Sofie had feared, had explained to the whole group that Sofie had lived in London for ten years.

"I'm sure your English is better than mine," the teacher had said with a little nervous laugh. "Please correct me if I make mistakes."

This, of course, had given Nathalie more to go on about, and although Sofie hadn't broached the subject herself, she heard comments like, "It's so typical for upper-class kids to try to be teacher's pet."

But actually, two good things had happened during the day. First of all, one of the boys in the class, in connection with Nathalie's comment in English class, had leaned over to Sofie and whispered, "Never mind her. She's always like that when there's somebody new. She'll give it up in a while."

Sofie had smiled thankfully at the boy and thought that maybe there was some hope for humanity after all.

Secondly, she hadn't really been able to stop thinking about those lovely eyes. Sofie realized that it was stupid. How could she think about a boy when everything was hopeless? But, she had thought, standing under the Norway maple during lunch break, maybe thinking about the cute boy was a way to push all the problems aside. A kind of escape from reality.

All day Sofie had walked around hoping to see him again. And every time she was in the big lobby, she looked around to try to learn where his locker was.

She didn't catch a glimpse of him until after the last class. He was throwing his backpack over his shoulder and saying something to his friend. They were laughing and looking happy in that way you do on a Friday afternoon when school is out and the weekend is stretched out before you.

Waiting for the school bus, Sofie had placed herself close to the blond boy and his friends. And if she hadn't misunderstood, his name was Adam.

Adam. Sofie tasted the name. It fit him very well.

And Adam and Sofie didn't sound too bad, either…

❁ ❁ ❁ ❁

"Hi! How've you been?" Isabelle came running across the yard. She seemed to be in a good mood, and Sofie noticed she was wearing new jeans.

"Not too good," Sofie admitted. "And you?"

Isabelle smiled.

"Great! Really wonderful! All the teachers seem great and the schedule is perfect. Our theory classes are in town, but we have almost as many classes in the stables at Jägersro. There are only two guys in our class… Poor saps, they're going to have a hard time!" Isabelle giggled. "One of them is pretty cute, actually."

As Isabelle talked, they walked toward the little stable, and just as the girls reached the door, Tina came out. It was four o'clock and Sofie guessed that the horse-minder was on her way home.

"Hi, girls! Thank goodness it's Friday, right?" Tina doffed her cap and ruffled her blonde hair.

"I wouldn't mind being in school all weekend," Isabelle said happily. "It's so much fun!"

"I'm glad to hear you enjoyed it!" Tina smiled. "But who would have thought anything else?"

46

Isabelle laughed and shrugged.

"No, I guess I would have been surprised myself if I hadn't liked the subjects. But I didn't know that the teachers would be this good... or that everybody in the class would be so fun!"

"No, right!" Tina turned to Sofie, and a little worried wrinkle appeared between her eyes. "And you? How was today? As bad?"

"Worse, actually." Sofie thought about Nathalie and felt anger bubbling up inside.

Isabelle covered her mouth with her hands.

"Oh! I'm *sorry*, Sofie. I've just kept babbling about myself without asking you. Tell me! What's happening?"

"Everything and nothing," Sofie said cryptically. "I'll tell you later..." She looked at the horse-minder. "But before you go home, I'd like to know about Speedy."

Tina's face brightened.

"Oh, there's probably no serious problem," she said.

"What did Andersson say?" Sofie asked.

"Speedy is probably just overworked." Tina put her cap on her head again. "That's not unusual with trotters. Several of our horses have had operations due to problems with their knees. Duke, for example..."

"Will Speedy have an operation?" Sofie looked at Tina in terror.

"An operation is the last step," Tina explained with a smile. "Hopefully, he'll react to the shot he had today and can start training again already next week. But of course he'll have to refrain from races for two weeks – there's a qualifying period of two weeks after this kind of treatment."

Isabelle had been standing silently next to Tina and Sofie as she listened to their conversation.

"I didn't even know Speedy was lame!" she burst out when Tina was done. She gave Sofie an offended look. "How could *you* know?"

Tina looked slightly amused.

"Well, it seems that somebody has had their mind elsewhere!"

"I came home late yesterday," Isabelle said, a little sheepishly. "Dad was at Solvalla and Mom and I hardly had time to say hi. Is he in much pain? I mean Speedy." She turned to Tina.

"Not while he's standing still," Tina said. "He can stay in the box for tonight, but I'm sure you can let him out in the paddock tomorrow afternoon."

"Come on, Sofie!" Isabelle tugged at her younger cousin's sleeve. "Let's go in and see him."

Tina smiled encouragingly at the girls and started walking toward the parking lot.

"You do that," she said. "The famous trotter might need to be perked up."

"See you Monday!" Isabelle called after Tina.

"Yes!" the horse-minder answered, smiling. "Have a nice weekend!"

Sofie turned and waved back at her as she jogged to keep up with Isabelle, who still tugged decisively at her sleeve.

"Hi, boy!" Isabelle walked straight up to Speedy's box. "Does your knee hurt, you poor thing?" She turned to Sofie. "If mom had told me about Speedy, I would have been here first thing last night."

Many of the more than forty horses at Humleby had been stabled there for years, and Sofie knew that Isabelle liked them all. But she also knew that her cousin, just like herself, had fallen completely for the beautiful chestnut with the white socks and thought about him as her special pet. Actually, it was Tina who took care of Speedy most of the time, but Sofie and Isabelle had worked in the little stable all summer and felt that they knew him almost as well as his minder.

"Maybe your mom couldn't get a word in," Sofie said, thinking about how geared up Isabelle must have been when she came home from her first day at school.

When Speedy heard the girls in the passageway, he put his head through the opening in the bars of the box.

"Well, maybe…" Isabelle scratched the chestnut between his ears and mumbled something to him. He answered by neighing softly.

"Tina was right," Sofie said, watching the gelding from a few feet away. "He actually does look kind of down. Sad, somehow…"

"Well, I'd be sad too, if I had to stand in a box all day and night."

Sofie remembered the apple that she had thrown in her backpack and taken with her after school.

"Look!" she said, holding the red apple up in front of Speedy. The gelding neighed again. "I promised you a treat next time I came!"

The chestnut trotter nuzzled the apple and Sofie held her palm out, making it possible for him to reach it. After less than half a minute, the apple was gone and Speedy put his head out again.

"I'm afraid that was it." Sofie opened the door to the box and went in to the gelding. She stroked his muscular neck and leaned her cheek against his shoulder. "You poor thing," she said. "Always bad luck!"

Isabelle stayed outside the box.

"Well, it's good to hear that he's probably just overworked," she said.

"Mmm," Sofie answered. She left the box and carefully closed the door behind her.

Tina and Isabelle didn't seem too worried about Speedy's bad knee. Obviously, they had seen lot of horses with the very same problem and were used to it. Sofie herself thought that it must be horrible to get an injection straight in your knee… And what if he didn't get well? That would ruin everything they had worked so hard for during the summer.

Worry kept nagging at her insides, but Sofie tried to push it away. She had to trust Tina and Isabelle. Worrying about school and Speedy at the same time was too much. It would be nice if she could forget about one of the two things.

"Now you must tell me about school!" Isabelle said as they slowly walked back toward the entrance.

"Well, it's hardly an uplifting tale," Sofie mumbled, stopping to see Tornado, who had his head out in the passageway.

"Well, never mind!" Isabelle put her hands to her sides and looked stern. "If anybody's mean to you, I promise I'll take care of them!"

Sofie smiled.

"So what are you going to do, anyway? Beat them up?"

Isabelle shook her head and smiled mysteriously.

"There are other ways!"

Sofie laughed and pulled her fingers through Tornado's black bangs.

Suddenly, life didn't feel quite as heavy as it had for the last few days. It was true that Speedy wasn't well, but he would soon get better. And maybe Isabelle could help her with Nathalie. Isabelle had gone to Sofie's school, and no doubt she knew a few things worth knowing. About the teachers and the students.

And, Sofie thought, maybe her older cousin would have some interesting information about a certain Adam.

❀ ❀ ❀ ❀

"Adam?" Isabelle's brow wrinkled. Suddenly her eyes glittered. "There's just one Adam there!"

"How do you know? There might be somebody new?" Sofie protested.

"Adam isn't a very common name," Isabelle persisted. "Is he short?"

"Well, at least not as tall as his friends…"

"And blond?"

"Yes, his hair is blond and curly."

"It *has* to be him!" Isabelle clapped her hands together in delight. "It has to be Adam Kempf!"

"What's so funny?" Sofie almost regretted telling her cousin about Adam. Isabelle was acting very strange.

"What do you think when you hear the name Kempf?" Isabelle asked, locking eyes with Sofie.

Sofie thought for a moment. Then she shrugged her shoulders.

"Nothing," she said. "Well, maybe… isn't there a politician by that name? Or maybe a high jumper?"

"Oh!" Isabelle smiled again. "I forgot that you're new to the horse business. Sven Kempf, Adam's dad, is one of my dad's biggest competitors! He's the one with the stable down by the crossroads."

"What?!" Sofie looked at Isabelle in confusion. "The stable where George usually is? The one right across from our house?"

"No, no…" Isabelle pointed out to the road. "The other direction. The first crossroads you come to if you drive north, past Humleby Farm."

Sofie still felt confused.

"But… Why did Adam get on the bus at the last stop? And why did he get off at the same place now, this afternoon?"

"Don't ask me!" Isabelle opened her palms. "Maybe he had a sleepover with a friend?"

Sofie tried to digest what she had learned. So, Adam's last name probably was Kempf, he lived less than a mile from Humleby – and his father was a horse trainer!

"Is Adam into horses?" she asked her cousin.

"He and I tried pony trotting when we were little. We were in the same group down at Jägersro. I think he drives big horses now, but I'm not sure. He might have grown tired of it."

Sofie couldn't really understand how anyone could grow tired of horses.

"Your dad and Adam's dad…"

"Yes?"

"Are they, like… enemies?"

"Ha, ha!" Isabelle laughed out loud. "No, not really. But they always bicker when they meet. Actually, I think they respect each other deeply. Sven has had some bad luck with his horses lately, but he's very good. At least, that's what Dad always says."

❀ ❀ ❀ ❀

As the two cousins perched on the bed in Isabelle's room, their parents sat on the glassed-in porch on the ground floor.

It was still Friday, but the afternoon had turned to evening. Maggie had invited her relatives to a spontaneous dinner and the Lindquists had immediately said yes.

By now, the meal was long over, and dusk was settling over Humleby. Maggie placed lanterns with tea-lights in the windows.

"I'm so glad Sofie is in a good mood tonight." Elizabeth

sipped from a glass and watched the dark shadows out in the yard.

Maggie found a box of matches and started lighting the tea lights, one by one.

"Has Sofie been down?" she asked.

"Down isn't the word..." Elizabeth sighed. "She's seemed heartbroken. And silent as a clam."

"You think it's about school?" Maggie put the matchbox back on the table and sat down on the old kitchen sofa with its new covering, next to her sister-in-law.

"Well, it started yesterday morning, so I guess so."

"It's always hard to start a new school and a completely new class." Maggie leaned over and took her glass. She sipped from it and held the glass in her hand.

"I just wish she'd talk about it!" Elizabeth looked despairing. "Sofie is hopeless that way. As soon as she feels troubled, she just clams up."

"You'll see, it'll get better by next week. She'll feel a little more at home by then."

Elizabeth sighed.

"You're probably right. I just hope that nobody's being mean to her."

"Why should anybody be mean to Sofie?" Stefan got into the conversation. "Sofie is sweet and doesn't make a spectacle of herself."

"You know how kids can be." Elizabeth turned to her husband. "You don't have to behave badly to get bullied. It's quite enough to be a little different. And being new in class can be enough to..." She fell silent.

"There's nothing wrong with Sofie!" Stefan put his arm around his wife. "Our daughter is always a little stand-offish when there are changes. She'll get used to it. In a few weeks, I'm sure our house will be full of her new buddies."

Elizabeth slowly nodded, without feeling totally convinced. Stefan could be so carefree sometimes. She often felt irritated when Stefan dismissed their daughter's problems as trifles. But then she thought that it might have to do with all the misery he saw in his job – and compared to leukemia, the first week at a new school wasn't really such a big problem.

It Never Rains, but It Pours

Sofie woke unnecessarily early on Saturday morning. It was just six o'clock, and she didn't have to be at Humleby Farm until seven. She spent five minutes tossing and turning in her bed, but it was impossible to go back to sleep. She threw her legs over the edge of the bed, sat there for a minute to let her head catch up and then walked over to the window.

When she opened the curtain the sharp morning light almost dazzled her, but she was able to make out Lisa and Mrs. Brown, standing close together on the other side of the paddock. The branches of a big tree were reaching out over them. The foliage made a green canopy, providing both shadow and shelter from the wind. The two mares seemed to have made this their favorite place – they often stood there, especially in the mornings.

A pheasant cock and his hen strutted around among the leftover food on the ground a good distance from the horses. The pheasants seemed to like the same food as horses, and George had said that several of the birds ate out of his hand.

A little black cat with a white collar snuck through the high grass at the edge of the paddock. The pheasants

55

looked up but didn't seem to care about either horses or cats. Sofie stood in the window for quite a while, watching the animals.

Suddenly, she had the urge to go out and say hello to the neighbor's horses. She felt that she had neglected them for a few days – and also, there was no point staying in bed when you felt perked-up and full of energy.

She wished that she could feel this energetic on Monday – when it was time to meet Nathalie and her crew again. Unfortunately, the chances of this happening were slim. But by now, at least she had *one* ace up her sleeve: Isabelle had given her younger cousin a good hint, and Sofie was almost a little curious about how Nathalie would react.

Also, she had to admit that she was curious to see if Adam would be on the school bus on Monday morning.

Sofie couldn't quite recognize herself.

Two months ago, she hadn't liked horses at all. Now, she loved them. As late as yesterday morning, she never thought about boys, but now her thoughts went to a guy named Adam Kempf, over and over.

What would happen next? Would she dye her hair blue? Or maybe start collecting stamps?

Sofie pulled on a T-shirt and a pair of socks. Then she sneaked downstairs and out to the porch where her stable clothes were hanging. Because of the nice weather, she just pulled her jeans on and let the windbreaker hang on its hook. She then jumped into her worn sneakers and walked out the porch door.

The morning was fresh and the grass still wet with dew. Sofie crossed the lawn and walked out on the village road. George's car was already parked out in the stable yard, but he was nowhere to be seen.

As soon as Lisa and Mrs. Brown discovered Sofie out in

the road, they came trotting from their resting place beneath the tree. The two mares were social and liked to "talk" to anybody who passed by. Now, they were waiting just inside the fence.

"Hi, girls!" Sofie greeted them, reaching her hand for Lisa's muzzle. The brown horse snorted and Lisa laughed. "Do I smell bad?" she asked.

"Iiihaaahaaa!" Mrs. Brown said, trying to join in, and Sofie patted her neck.

"You're so fine," she praised them. The mares seemed to enjoy her attention and Sofie kept patting them as she softly talked about whatever came into her mind.

Sofie caught herself feeling that it was very nice to be up this early on a Saturday morning. The silence was striking. The only sound was the muffled noise from a few trucks passing on the highway, far from the paddocks of Humleby Farm. Maybe it was trucks from southern Europe, going north.

The pheasant cock screamed over by the fodder, and Sofie suspected he wanted more food.

"Take it easy!" she yelled to the bird. "George is on his way!"

At that moment there was a violent crash inside the stable on the other side of the road. The crash was followed by a scream that echoed hauntingly in the silence that had been so alluring.

Sofie jumped and felt her arms go prickly. *What* was that?

Lisa and Mrs. Brown started back at Sofie's sudden movement. Their ears were directed to where the unexpected sound had come from and they treaded uneasily in place.trod"I'm sorry!" Sofie said to the horses. "I'll be back. I just have to see what happened!"

She ran across the village road toward the white stable. Both doors were open and she took the first one.

"Hello?" Sofie called. She gingerly stepped into the passageway. "Is anybody here?"

No answer. The stable was silent and still, apart from a few muffled neighs and the rustle of hooves moving in the straw.

Maybe she had just imagined somebody screaming?

"Hello?" she shouted again.

Her eyes needed a few seconds to get used to the subdued light in the stable, but just as she heard the soft moaning she saw him.

George was lying on the floor under the loft. One leg was bent at a strange angle, and his eyes were closed.

Sofie ran up to the old man.

"George!" she called. "What happened?"

"The loft…" George mumbled. "I fell…"

Oh, no! Sofie thought. *I have to call an ambulance. Should I go home or out in the yard? What if he dies?*

Just then Thomas, the owner of the farm, came running into the stable. His hair stood on end and he was only wearing briefs and clogs. Normally, Sofie would have thought that it was unbearably embarrassing to meet the neighbor in this scant outfit, but she was too panicked to care about his clothes.

"What happened?" Thomas asked, looking as if he just woke up. "Are you tearing the place down?"

Sofie pointed to where George was lying.

"I think he fell down from the loft!" she said. "I was standing by the paddock and heard this terrible crash, and when I came in he was just lying there…" Sofie had to catch her breath before she could go on. "W-what should we do?"

"I'll stay here with George while you go get your dad!" Thomas said, hurrying up to the old man.

Sofie was immensely grateful that Thomas had woken.

She was also glad that he was able to think in spite of his sudden awakening – she hadn't even thought about the fact that her dad was a doctor and very close by.

"Okay!" She turned on her heels and ran for the red brick house at top speed.

Lisa and Mrs. Brown stood at the fence, watching the running girl.

❀ ❀ ❀

"Dad!" Sofie screamed, tearing the porch door open. "Dad! Wake up!"

Stefan sat up in bed.

"What!?" He rubbed his eyes. "Is there a fire?"

Sofie told the entire story as she egged her dad on by waving her arms wildly close to his face.

"Calm down!" Stefan told his daughter as he put his pants on. "If you keep on like that, you'll start hyperventilating – and I don't want to have to take care of two patients on a Saturday morning."

He grabbed a black bag that stood behind the door of the bedroom and asked Sofie to grab the cell phone that was on the night table.

"If we have to call an ambulance," he explained.

Three minutes later, father and daughter Lindquist were standing in the weak light in the stable. Sofie was panting after running home and back.

Thomas sat on the floor, talking softly to George. George was white as a sheet. Sofie thought that his face looked almost transparent.

"Good thing you could make it so fast." Thomas looked up at Stefan. "He seems to be in a bad way."

"Is he conscious?" Sofie's dad sank down on his knees next to the old man and Thomas got to his feet, relieved that an expert was taking charge.

"Yes, but only just…"

"We might as well call an ambulance now… I'll do what I can for the time being. If we're lucky, he's just broken his leg and gotten a concussion."

Stefan gestured for Sofie to give the cell phone to Thomas, and while Thomas called 911, Sofie crouched next to her dad. She bent down and patted George's cheek.

"You're going to be okay," she said. "My dad's here now, and the ambulance will be here to pick you up in a minute."

George opened his eyes and looked at Sofie with something that was close to desperation.

"The horses…" he whispered. "Somebody has to… My horses!"

Sofie knew exactly what George meant.

"Don't worry," she said quickly. "I'll take care of Lisa and Mrs. Brown while you're at the hospital."

"B-but…" George wanted to say something else but couldn't find the words. The old man looked so helpless that Sofie wanted to hug him.

"I promise I'll take care of them!" she said. "They're going to be fine – and you'll soon be back in the stable again."

Stefan quickly glanced at his daughter. It was a glance that seemed to mean that he wanted to talk to her in private – later.

Sofie ignored her dad and went on, "Now don't worry about the horses, George. Make sure you rest and get well instead."

Sofie realized that she was babbling mostly to allay her own fears. George seemed harder and harder to reach, and his leg looked as if it had fallen off and then been screwed on the wrong way.

She remembered a plastic doll that Jojo had given her when they were five. The doll often lost her legs, and the girls used to giggle hysterically when Sofie put them on backwards. Sofie shuddered.

Just then, George lifted the arm that wasn't underneath him and searched for Sofie's hand. She took the big, calloused hand in her own and pressed it.

"Now rest," she said.

The old man seemed calmer.

"Thank you," he said, closing his eyes.

Suddenly, they heard sirens down the hill and Thomas ran out front to make sure that the ambulance didn't go the wrong way. A minute later, the yellow car pulled up in front of the white stuccoed building and three men jumped onto the yard.

At a distance, Sofie watched the paramedics carefully place George on a stretcher while Stefan gave them a short account of what probably had happened and what he himself had done.

Less than five minutes later, the ambulance turned back toward the town. Thomas, Stefan and Sofie stood outside the stable, watching it disappear behind the trees.

"Gosh!" Thomas exclaimed after a moment of silence. "What a morning!" He turned to Stefan. "You think he'll make it?"

Stefan nodded.

"Yes… I'm sure they can mend the broken bone. The only thing that worried me was his drowsiness… But as I said…" Stefan put his hand to his sides and pulled his shoulders back to stretch his back. "I hope, believe, that it's just a bad concussion," he went on. "But George is no spring chicken, so it might be some time before he gets well."

"May I treat you to a cup of strong coffee?" Thomas

62

asked. "I'll just slip into something more… presentable."
He looked down at his briefs and smiled guiltily.

"Why not?" Stefan smiled back at him. "A cup of coffee would really be nice."

"Ask your wife too!" Thomas looked up. "It seems she's already on her way."

Elizabeth came running along the village road, her nightgown flapping around her legs.

Stefan raised his hand and waved.

"Good morning, dear!" He called.

"I'll get out of here," Thomas said. "I'll wake my wife up and – as I said – get dressed. You just go on in the house. In five minutes, I'll be decent. And Sofie is welcome too, of course!"

❀ ❀ ❀ ❀

Sofie stood in the stable yard, listening with one ear as Stefan told his wife what had happened. Elizabeth accompanied her husband's tale with small exclamations of "Oh!" and "I say!" and when Stefan was done she turned to Sofie, saying, "But honey, how are you? It must have been a terrible shock for you to find George lying on the floor in there!"

Sofie nodded absently.

She had just realized that she had promised somebody that she would take care of two horses indefinitely. Two horses that needed to be cared for and fed morning and evening…

The horses at Humleby Farm she could take care of with no problem now. She knew the routines and found her way everywhere. And at Humleby Farm, she was never alone.

But as Stefan and Elizabeth stood talking about the dramatic incidents of the morning, Sofie realized that she didn't have even the faintest idea how George took care of his horses.

What did he feed them? She had seen that they got hay, but they had to have something else besides. And when she looked around the stable yard, she realized that she didn't even know where their food *was!*

George had built a little shelter for the horses to stand under when it rained. But they couldn't be outside if it poured for days? Or could they?

"Oh!" Elizabeth said, looking at her watch. "It's quarter past seven. Shouldn't you be at Humleby Farm by now, Sofie?"

Trouble

Sofie stared at her mom as thoughts raced around in her head. She had totally forgotten that she was supposed to work today!

"I just asked if you shouldn't be at Humleby Farm by now," Elizabeth repeated. "It's after seven. Sofie?" Elizabeth waved her hand in front of Sofie's empty eyes. "Are you all right?"

"Um… yeah…" Sofie managed to collect the thoughts in her overheated brain and made a quick decision. "Dad, may I borrow your cell phone?" She decisively put her hand out. Stefan put his hand in his pocket and found his phone.

"Sure, as long as you don't call Jojo and talk for forty minutes. Ha, ha!" He laughed loudly at his own joke.

Sofie snatched the phone from her dad's hand and quickly entered the number to Isabelle's cell phone. Her cousin answered after four signals.

"Hello?" Isabelle sounded out of breath.

"Hi, it's me. Are you up?"

"What do you think? I'm in the stable. Where are *you*?"

Sofie could hear Isabelle walking along the passageway as she talked. She drew a deep breath before she went on.

"You see, there's been an accident and…"

Isabelle inhaled sharply.

65

"What? Is it bad? Are you hurt?" She sounded worried.

"I'm alright," Sofie hurried to say. "It's George... You know, the old man who has his horses in the paddock next to our house."

"What's that got to do with you?"

"It's a long story..." Sofie debated whether she should tell Isabelle now or later, but decided to wait. "I just have to give his horses some food and water," she said. "Is that okay?"

"Sure..." Isabelle hesitated a little. "Come as soon as you can, you know where I am." She gave a little sigh.

"Thank you, great! See you!" Sofie ended the call, gave the phone to her dad and then ran into the stable.

For a few minutes, she just stood in the passageway, looking around helplessly. Where was the fodder? There were a few sacks and cans in a corner – but she didn't know what was in them. Sofie opened one of the sacks and felt with her hand. It smelled and looked like concentrated feed...

Aside from George, two other amateur trainers rented in this stable. They all kept their fodder in the same place, so it was hard for Sofie to decide which sacks and cans belonged to whom. She could feel panic grabbing her. A wave of heat rushed through her body – from her head and all the way down to her toes.

Suddenly she realized that Thomas might know.

"Sofie?" Elizabeth poked her head through the door. "What are you doing? Aren't you going to Humleby Farm?"

"Soon!" Sofie quickly turned around. She had already run through the stable and was on her way out to the yard. When she came to the house, she impatiently banged on the red door.

Five seconds later, Thomas was standing in the door, now dressed in jeans and a T-shirt. Sofie could hear his wife working in the kitchen.

"Oh, are you in such a hurry for breakfast!" Thomas smiled. "Come on in. Julia is getting everything in order."

Sofie wildly shook her head.

"It isn't… It isn't about breakfast…" she panted. "The horses… George's horses have to have some food. Do you know what he usually gives them and where I can find it?"

Thomas slapped his forehead.

"Thank you, Sofie!" he exclaimed. "I must have been more shocked than I thought… Goodness! Of course we have to feed the horses. Julia!" He turned and called toward the kitchen. "I'll just help Sofie with something, and we'll be right back!"

The noises stopped for a moment and an "Okay" was heard from the kitchen. Thomas put his feet in his worn black clogs and followed Sofie back to the stable.

Sofie silently watched as Thomas rummaged around the sacks, buckets and bottles.

"I think George feeds his horses oats mixed with oil," he explained. "He probably also gives them vitamins and salt." He nodded to a jar of salt, standing on a bench.

"Doesn't he give them hay?" Sofie asked, right before realizing what a silly question that was. After all, George had fallen from the hayloft.

"Yes, right, of course," Thomas said. "Morning and evening." He looked around and went on, "George mixes his fodder in those buckets." He pointed to two small white plastic buckets, standing on the floor next to one of the sacks of oats. "But to be honest, I have no idea how much he gives them of one or the other. And maybe they shouldn't have the same amount of fodder either… Lisa is a little smaller than Mrs. Brown."

Sofie looked at her neighbor unhappily.

"What should we do?"

"I'll try to reach George today," Thomas said. "For now, we'll just have to give them some oats and hay. It won't kill them if they don't get the exact amount of feed on just one occasion. The most important thing is that they get something to eat." He scooped oats into both buckets and started mixing it up with oil.

Sofie thought of Isabelle. She wondered what was happening in the little stable and if her cousin was in a bad mood by now. Sofie was already more than half an hour late, and she realized she wouldn't be at Humleby Farm until around nine o'clock.

"Climb up to the loft and see if you can manage to pull a bale of hay out," Thomas suggested. "Just throw it down in the passageway. There's a wheelbarrow there that you can put the hay in."

Sofie awoke from her thoughts.

"Right!" She turned on her heels and went for the ladder.

"And don't fall down, now!" Thomas called after her. "No more accidents today, please!"

"I'll try," Sofie answered as she approached the loft on the rickety ladder.

❋ ❋ ❋ ❋

A short time later, Sofie and Thomas crossed the village road with a wheelbarrow and two buckets of oats.

Sofie raked up the remains of the old hay and sprinkled a little new hay in the middle of the paddock as Thomas poured the feed in the mares' feeders. Then, he showed Sofie where the hose was and let her fill the big tub with fresh water.

Lisa and Mrs. Brown seemed satisfied with what they got, and when Thomas and Sofie left the horses they stood munching their hay as if nothing had happened. The black tails waved to keep persistent flies away and their coats shone in the sun.

68

"Thanks for reminding me," Thomas said as he carefully closed the gate to the paddock. "I'm afraid those poor horses would have had to wait quite a while for their breakfast if you hadn't." He suddenly looked troubled. "I actually don't know what to do now. I don't have the time to take care of them myself. I leave home at seven, and when I come home there's always lots of stuff to fix at my own place…"

"I promised George that I'd take care of them," Sofie said, smiling.

Her feelings of panic had subsided and she was beginning to believe that she would be able to cope with her task. If Thomas could just get hold of George, everything would work out.

"How kind of you." Thomas smiled back. "Then you'll have to get up at the crack of dawn for a while, too!"

Sofie's smile got faint. She hadn't even thought about the fact that the school bus came to pick her up at a quarter past seven on weekday mornings. After some quick mental calculations, she realized what this meant: She would have to get up right after five o'clock every morning to have time for the horses!

And she could forget about getting rest on the weekends. She was supposed to be at Humleby Farm at seven…

In the next moment, she thought that George would probably be up and about by the end of the week. It would only be a matter of a few days, she calmed herself. She simply would manage this. She had promised to.

Sofie placed the wheelbarrow next to the stable wall and went in.

"Is it alright if I leave now?" she asked.

Thomas, who had been rinsing out and putting back the white plastic buckets in place, looked at her with surprise.

69

"Aren't you coming in for breakfast? You have to be starved."

"No time," Sofie explained. "I'm late as it is. I'll take a piece of fruit to Humleby Farm."

"Okay, suit yourself. But don't blame me if you die from starvation."

Sofie laughed.

"I promise I won't come back to haunt you!"

❀ ❀ ❀ ❀

Isabelle didn't look very happy when Sofie came running into the little stable at five past nine. She placed a manure fork into her younger cousin's hand, saying, "Here! You take care of the boxes."

Then she disappeared through the stable door.

By now, Sofie was getting used to Isabelle's hot temper. And she had also learned that her older cousin seldom stayed angry for long. Sofie was sure that Isabelle would be more understanding when she heard that Lisa and Mrs. Brown were dependent on Sofie's help. Animal suffering was the worst thing Isabelle could imagine.

Her cousin had taken out the four horses that stayed inside at night, and Sofie started mucking out Champion's box. She methodically worked her way along the passageway as images from the morning chased each other inside her head.

The images were nasty. To see George lying on the floor with his leg in that unnatural angle had been a shock, and it wasn't until now that she began taking in what had actually happened. She wildly hoped that the old man hadn't suffered any internal damage and that he'd soon be well again.

When she had worked for a while, hunger began to be a problem. Up till now she had more or less been able to

70

suppress her pangs of hunger, but now her stomach was positively aching. The apple she had wolfed down on her way to Humleby Farm didn't seem to ease her hunger, quite the contrary.

To drive away thoughts of food Sofie took a little break and went up to her chestnut favorite. Speedy put his head out through the open hatch and neighed softly when he saw her.

"Hi, boy!" Sofie put her hand out and pulled her fingers through his thick, golden-yellow bangs. "How's your knee today?" she asked and bent down to look at the horse's leg.

"It seems a lot better today." Isabelle was back in the stable, and she sounded in a better mood than before. "I think we can take him out to the paddock after lunch," she said, putting down a plastic basket with clean leg wraps on the floor just inside the door.

Sofie turned and smiled at her cousin.

"Great! I've been worried."

Isabelle shrugged.

"Most trotters have problems with their legs sometime in their lives. Compare it to people who train a lot. Many top athletes get overworked..."

"I know." Sofie looked at Speedy again. "But I think he's had enough problems. His injury after the derby, the owner who didn't take care of him, colic..."

"Well, I guess you're right." Isabelle went into Sky's box. "Sky is going to do a fast job[3] with Ewa and Lucia," she said, leading the dark brown gelding out in the passageway. She tied him up and went over to the tin cupboards, where she picked out a bridle and harness. "It's about time to check out his form. He'll be starting in a race next Saturday," she explained.

3 A fast job means that the horse is driven at full speed on a track, to test its condition and judge if it's ready for a race. Often at least two horses are driven at the same time, to make them compete as hard as possible.

Sofie nodded.

"I'm sorry I was so late today," she said. She thought she might as well clear the air at once.

Her older cousin looked at her across Sky's muscular neck.

"That's all right. What happened?"

As Isabelle put the harness on Sky and carefully tightened it, Sofie told her everything that had happened that morning, from finding George on the floor to feeding the old man's mares.

"Wow!" Isabelle exclaimed when Sofie was done. "What luck that your dad was home!"

Sofie grinned.

"Yes, sometimes he actually has his uses…"

Isabelle loosened the reins and led Sky toward the stable door. Just before walking out into the yard, she stopped and turned.

"So *you* are going to take care of those two horses now?" she asked.

Sofie nodded.

"All by yourself?"

"I'm just going to feed them and so on…"

"Feed them and so on?" Isabelle repeated Sofie's words and rolled her eyes. "You of all people should know by now that taking care of horses is a big job. It's not like owning a goldfish, you know."

"Don't you think I'm up to it?" Sofie locked eyes with her cousin.

"Well, yes…" Isabelle was thoughtful. "But it's a big responsibility. And where will you find the time?"

Sofie sighed.

"You sound just like my parents!" she exclaimed. "And by the way, it's only for a couple of days. The horses are outside almost all of the time, so there isn't much mucking out to do. And George only grooms them when he's going to drive them."

Isabelle smiled. "Okay, I stand corrected." She walked out into the yard, where Ewa was waiting in the long wagon behind Lucia, but then she put her head back in through the door again.

"Sofie!"

"Yeah?"

"Come here and hold Sky while I get a wagon!"

Sofie walked out obediently and took Sky's reins. She was unable to refrain from giving her cousin a sour look. She had hoped for some support from Isabelle – at least a couple of encouraging words – but it seemed she had been wrong.

It felt good that Thomas, at least, was thankful for her help. He didn't seem to doubt her ability. And neither did George.

Sofie was adamant, she wouldn't let the old man down.

Working Like a Horse

"Watch it!" Sofie couldn't help hissing at Lisa, who had placed herself right behind the gate and now refused to move.

Sofie didn't dare walk into the paddock when the mare was so close to the gate. She was scared to death that one of the horses would run away. If George heard that something like that had happened, he'd probably run away from the hospital, and she didn't think that would be very good.

It was quarter to six on Sunday morning, and the sun was rising slowly. Sofie could feel autumn sneaking around. The air felt fresh, almost cold, and there were still thin veils of fog above the dewy grass of the paddock.

When her alarm went off at five, Sofie had been sure that she had programmed it wrong and that it was still the middle of the night. Her eyelids had been as heavy as lead and her entire body had just wanted one single thing: to remain in bed.

What had finally gotten her to her feet – after snoozing for about fifteen minutes – was the thought of poor George, who couldn't see his horses. She knew that they were everything to him.

"Come on, Lisa. Move over now, so I can get in and give you your food. I'm sure you're hungry, right, honey?"

Sofie made an effort to speak softly and calmly. She knew that yelling wouldn't get her anywhere. "I know you miss George," she went on kindly. "He'll be back soon, but for now, I'm the one in charge, okay?"

Lisa didn't even flutter an ear. She stubbornly stayed put, eyes wide, and Sofie had the feeling that Lisa was ready to fling herself out of the paddock as soon as the gate opened.

Mrs. Brown had trotted up to the fence and placed herself next to her buddy. She stretched her neck, trying to reach the white buckets.

George's horses never used to be this stupid! Sofie guessed that the mares could sense that she was nervous and stressed and planned to use it to their advantage. They were probably eager to do some sightseeing in the neighborhood – something that George would never allow.

"So, you don't want any food, right?" Frustration was creeping in, and Sofie glared angrily at the little horse. It was hard to stay calm when her workday was quickly drawing closer.

Sofie had left Humleby Farm at four on Sunday afternoon, taken a shower at home, wolfed down dinner, rushed out to Lisa and Mrs. Brown, given them food and water, had another shower and fallen asleep almost before her head hit the pillow.

A few times, her parents had tried to discuss with her whether it was smart to take care of two horses – when she already had a job at Humleby Farm. But by talking incessantly, she had managed to avoid the subject. For now…

"Lisa, please!" Sofie asked. *"Please!"*

When the little brown horse still didn't move, Sofie realized she had to take charge. She put the buckets on

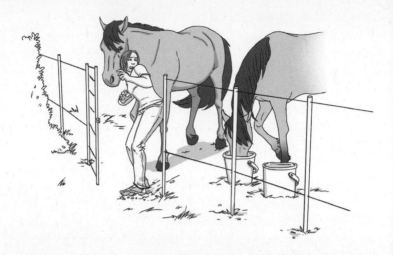

the ground, opened the gate and cautiously but decisively pushed Lisa away with her shoulder. The mare was quick, but Sofie managed to close the gate at the last second – before somebody got out.

Mrs. Brown immediately put her muzzle down in one of the buckets, and Sofie let her eat. It was no use walking over to her feeder with the little food that was left. Instead, she went to empty the other bucket into Lisa's feeder.

"I'll be right back!" she said, patting Lisa's neck. "I'll just get some hay."

This is going to work out fine, Sofie told herself when she crossed the village road to get the wheelbarrow which she had already filled with hay. It's just a matter of taking charge!

❋ ❋ ❋

At exactly seven AM Sofie walked into the dark little stable at Humleby Farm. Unlike yesterday, she had had the time to eat breakfast between her chores. This made her morning a little better, but she had eaten too fast and could now feel the yogurt sloshing around in her stomach.

The horses seemed as tired as she felt. Everybody but Rocky was standing in their boxes, heads hanging and eyelids half-closed.

Rocky was his usual self, which meant that he was standing chewing the bars of the box. The dark brown stallion seemed to think he could chew his way out if he just worked hard enough.

"Stop that!" Sofie couldn't help laughing, but she didn't dare put her hand out and pat him. That felt like challenging destiny.

Tina and Isabelle were good with the unruly stallion, and Sofie admired them for that. She thought that from now on, she would try to study her fellow workers in the stable a little more closely. The morning's feeding of Lisa and Mrs. Brown had given her an unwelcome reminder that she was still a beginner when it came to horses. She needed to learn a *lot* more about how to act in different situations.

"Good morning!" Isabelle suddenly stood in the stable door. Sofie's cousin looked irritatingly perky. As usual, her blonde hair was tied in a ponytail and she was dressed in a pale pink T-shirt and her usual stable jeans. "So, how did you do with George's horses?" she asked.

"Great," Sofie lied. "They're so nice."

"That's good! I really admire you for helping that old boy. Is he still working as a school janitor?"

Sofie didn't like Isabelle calling George an old boy. It sounded condescending. She was well aware that most of the people working at Humleby Farm looked down at George and the other amateur trainers in the vicinity. Several times, she had heard the staff here, even Tommy and Maggie, talking about the amateurs as if they were ignorant and almost a little stupid.

But even Sofie, who hadn't worked with horses for long,

could see that everybody, professionals and amateurs alike, were driven by their interest in trotting and their love for horses. The biggest difference was that the pros had more money, and therefore more options.

"I think he does," Sofie answered. "But I didn't see him last week."

Isabelle took Rocky's bridle off its hook.

"I think we'll have to let this rascal out first," she said, opening the door to the stallion's box. "He's really nuts!"

"Watch it," Sofie warned her. "He might understand what you're saying."

Isabelle giggled.

"If he were smart enough to understand what we're saying, he wouldn't be cribbing on his bars all day long." She put the bridle on swiftly. Rocky neighed, sounding upset, but it was probably more from habit than in protest.

"Can you take Oh My Glory out?" Isabelle asked as she headed for the passageway.

"Okay." Sofie took Oh My Glory's bridle from the hook next to the gelding's box. "You want me to take Champion, too?"

"If you want to. Then we'll only have Tornado to worry about," her older cousin said, leading Rocky out into the yard.

❀ ❀ ❀ ❀

Sofie walked back to the stable, mucking out while Isabelle led Tornado to his paddock. Fifteen minutes later, Speedy's beautiful figure stood in the doorway.

"Hello, prince!" Sofie ran up to the chestnut and patted him. "You really are the most beautiful horse in the world, do you know that?" Speedy bent down, nuzzling Sofie's pockets. "I'm sorry. I didn't have time to bring any treats for you today. I'll try to find a carrot as soon as the boxes are done…"

Sofie suddenly fell quiet when she discovered a big worry wrinkle between Isabelle's eyebrows. Isabelle tied the chestnut gelding up in the passageway with quick movements.

"What is it? Did something happen?" Sofie suddenly felt ill at ease.

"He's lame again," Isabelle said in a clipped tone. "I have to get Dad."

"Oh no!" Sofie looked down. She couldn't see anything on Speedy's knee, but she did notice that the chestnut avoided putting weight on his right foreleg. "Drat and double drat," she exclaimed.

"I'll be right back!" Isabelle said, running out of the stable.

Sofie stayed next to the beautiful horse. She had a feeling that whatever Tommy had to say, it wasn't something that she'd like hearing. She leaned her cheek against the gelding's neck.

"Poor you!" she whispered. "Poor, poor you. You've had some real bad luck."

As if he understood what she was saying, Speedy let out something that sounded like a loud sigh. He stood very still beside her and Sofie put her nose into his golden mane. "Poor you," she repeated.

Five minutes later, Isabelle rushed back into the stable, followed closely by Tommy. Tommy said a quick hello to Sofie and immediately bent down to examine Speedy's knee. He carefully lifted the gelding's leg and bent the knee back and forth. The chestnut didn't seem to like this and neighed loudly.

Sofie couldn't work. She stood a few feet away from Speedy and his trainer, silently praying that Tommy would dismiss the horse's lameness as something perfectly normal and say that everything was all right. Just yesterday, she reminded herself, Isabelle had said that there was nothing strange about trotters having problems with their legs.

Tommy talked soothingly to Speedy as he felt the knee with his fingers. Sofie thought about the fantastic race that the chestnut had run at his home track just a few days ago. He had been magnificent – he had run like the wind along the track – and everybody had praised him.

At the time, Tommy, sporting a big smile, had said that Speedy Legend was "coming along." That they were seeing the beginning of something big. But now, when her uncle rose upon examining the gelding's knee, he didn't look at all happy.

Sofie swallowed and her stomach tied into a knot. Just like everybody else around Speedy, she had hoped for a fall filled with races and just as many victories. It would be so unfair if everything ended before it even began.

"It seems the shot didn't help," Tommy said, confirming Sofie's worries. "We'll have to take him to the clinic and let Andersson X-ray his knee. I'll call him right away, and hopefully we can get in there first thing tomorrow morning."

❀ ❀ ❀ ❀

For the rest of the day, the two cousins worked in silence. The silence wasn't embarrassing – it wasn't the kind of silence one might find when people have fallen out with each other and just wish that the other person would say something. It was a silence caused by two girls deep in thought.

Sofie was thinking about Speedy. She wanted so much for things to work out for him. Somehow, it felt like her own happiness depended on how Speedy was doing. He was the one who had made her feel at home at Humleby Farm, and it was thanks to him that she had started getting interested in horses.

When Speedy won the race last week, she had felt that her happiness was complete. Jojo had been there. Isabelle and Tina had been there. Tommy and Maggie and her own parents had been there. Everybody had been there, and everybody had been so happy.

It had been an unbelievable feeling to experience Speedy's comeback with the people who had helped him make it, friends and acquaintances.

And Speedy had seemed so strong and proud.

Sofie sighed deeply and kept working. She wondered if Tommy had managed to get a hold of Andersson and what the vet could have said, but she never had a chance to ask. Tommy didn't show up again, and Maggie just quickly stuck her head inside the little stable and told them that Speedy should stay in his box during the night.

By coincidence, most of the horses at Humleby Farm had this Sunday off, which meant that the girls had finished all their chores by two thirty. In no hurry, they put fly-blankets on Sky, Lucky and Star and then led the horses out in the yard to take them to their paddocks.

The cool morning had turned into a hot summer day. The August sun was high on a blue sky, and the ears of corn on the stalks out in the few fields that hadn't been harvested yet shone like gold in the light. But Sofie didn't see any of this, since she was still thinking of Speedy.

When they had walked for a while, Isabelle suddenly said, "Actually, Speedy might not be so bad off."

Sofie had almost forgotten that she wasn't the only one who was worried. She felt a little better when she realized she wasn't alone.

"Your dad didn't seem that hopeful," she said.

Isabelle sighed.

"I guess I'm mostly trying to cheer myself up." She

thought for a moment and then went on, sounding a little more self-assured, "But if they don't find anything in the X-rays, maybe he's just overworked after all…"

"We can always hope." Sofie reined in Lady, who had seen an approaching danger in the form of a kid on a tricycle. It was Jack's little sister Jennifer, out with her mother. "Easy, easy," Sofie calmed the nervously trampling horse. "I know she looks scary," she joked, "but it's only Jennifer, and she doesn't bite. I promise."

Jennifer and her mother stopped at the side of the road and Lady started walking forward again. Sofie waved to her neighbors.

The girls crossed the road and walked in between the paddocks. When they arrived, Sofie unsnapped Lady's lead rein and let the horse run off along the inside of the fence. Star seemed to be in an unusually good mood and happily gamboled when Isabelle let her out in the lush grass. Sofie laughed and closed the gate.

She looked at the two trotters one last time before she walked out onto the little gravel path where Isabelle stood waiting with Sky. Just as she turned around, she realized something: Blankets! George's horses should have fly-blankets too!

Sofie had never thought about either fly-blankets or eye and ear protection when she fed Lisa and Mrs. Brown in the morning. And the more she thought about it now, the more she remembered how both horses almost always had blankets and fly masks on hot summer days.

Help! What if they were half eaten by bugs by now?

Plain Speaking

When Sofie ran toward the neighbor's horse paddock after her day at Humleby Farm she saw, to her surprise, two brown mares with fly-blankets and masks neatly in place.

Who had done it? Was George back already?

"Hello there!" A brusque voice from the stable made her turn.

In the door of the storeroom stood an elderly man with gray, bushy hair and a cap.

"Are you the one taking care of George's horses?" he called.

Sofie nodded and crossed the road. She recognized the man. He was one of the other two amateur trainers who, like George, rented boxes in Thomas's stable. This man's horses stayed in a couple of the smaller paddocks on the other side of the farm, and Sofie had seen him from a distance almost every day during the summer.

She had never talked to him before. He didn't seem as companionable as George, and in spite of that Sofie could see quite clearly, when she walked up to him, that he wasn't in the best mood this Sunday afternoon.

"Do you know anything about horses?" the older man rumbled when Sofie stood in front of him.

"W-well… um… a little," Sofie stammered, feeling irritated that her voice sounded so thin.

The man gave her a long lecture about why fly masks were important and then cross-examined her about what she had given George's horses that morning. Sofie was deeply thankful that Thomas had called last night and told her what to feed them. He hadn't spoken to George, but had happened to find a note among the sacks out in the stable.

The cap man went on about fly masks for a while, and Sofie felt terribly disappointed with herself for making that mistake. She was glad that the horses hadn't suffered during the day, but she was very irritated that it wasn't thanks to her. She *knew* that they needed fly masks! She had just forgotten about it…

Sofie almost told the man with the bushy hair that *he* was welcome to take care of Lisa and Mrs. Brown – since he seemed so immensely knowledgeable. But before she found a moment to say this, the cap man announced that he, in light of Sofie's lack of knowledge, should *offer* to take care of George's horses, but that he really didn't have the time to care for any animals besides his own. Then he turned on his heels and left Sofie alone in the yard.

She hated being criticized, and a little voice deep inside her told her that she was out of her league.

But Sofie decided to try to shake off the criticism. Actually, she had neither let the horses out nor made them starve. And she refused to listen to that stubborn voice. She had *promised* George she would take care of Lisa and Mrs. Brown – and she was going to show him and Isabelle that she could do it!

It was just six thirty on Sunday night when Sofie started longing for her bed. Her entire body ached with exhaustion and just the thought that she had to get up just after five AM made her feel nauseous. During dinner she could hardly grip her knife and fork, and she had to muster all her energy to keep from putting her cheek on the table and resting just a little.

Sofie and Elizabeth were dining alone, since Stefan had been playing golf at a course outside town and had gotten stuck in a traffic jam on the freeway. Elizabeth mildly tried to get her daughter to understand that she had taken on too much, but Sofie said that she was too tired to talk about it.

"There you are!" Elizabeth called out in triumph. "You're too tired to even talk! So how are you going to manage school?"

"It's just a matter of a couple of days…" Sofie put her arm around her mother and kissed her on the tip of her nose, which was a sure-fire way to calm her down. "Is it okay if I excuse myself now?" Sofie asked. "I have to go to bed."

"Sure." Elizabeth rose with her and started collecting the dishes. "But still, we have to solve this situation. I'll talk to Dad when he comes home."

"I'll talk to Dad," Sofie mumbled, making an ugly face as she walked up the stairs. It was the same old story. She wondered why her parents always had to agree when it came to decisions about her. It was probably their way of outmaneuvering her – two against one.

She had just gotten her pajamas on and threw herself down on the bed when there was a knock on her door. A second later, the door opened and Stefan walked in with decisive steps.

"Why do you bother knocking if you're just going to walk right in anyway?" Sofie lay on the bed with her eyes closed. She knew what was coming.

"You have to find somebody else to take care of George's horses," Stefan began. He seldom sugared his messages with unnecessary phrases.

"There isn't anybody," Sofie quickly said. She still hadn't opened her eyes. "Thomas doesn't have the time, the old men in his stable don't want to. And as I told Mom, George will be back soon!"

"Well, that's the problem, actually," Stefan said. He sat down on the edge of the bed. "I just called the hospital to check on things, and –"

Sofie opened her eyes and turned her head so that she could see her dad.

"What did they say?" she interrupted. "When will he be out?"

"He'll probably be out of there next week," Stefan said, "but it –"

"Great! So what's the problem?"

Stefan sighed.

"Sofie, please, would you let me make my point?" He went on, "George was lucky. He had a minor concussion and made it without internal bleeding. It's true, he'll be discharged next week, but he'll be in a cast from his upper thigh all the way down. George will have to lie still, and he won't be able to walk without crutches for months."

Sofie quickly sat up in the bed.

"What!?"

"You heard me. His leg is broken in several places, and George won't be able to take care of his horses for quite a long time."

Sofie could feel the air being pressed out of her. It was one thing to work hard for a week or two, but she wouldn't be able to keep up the tempo of the last two days for the whole fall! Weekdays might be okay; many people took care of horses both mornings and evenings, but to work double every weekend on top of that… Even Sofie could see that it was impossible.

"Maybe George knows somebody…" she began.

"Yes!" It was Stefan's turn to interrupt in the middle of a sentence. "We'll have to ask around. Can't you ask Isabelle if she can help you until we find somebody else?"

Sofie threw herself down again.

"She'd never do that."

Stefan raised his eyebrows.

"Why is that? She's so nice and helpful…"

Sofie didn't have the stamina to explain that Isabelle thought George was a bungler, and that she herself wanted to prove to her cousin that she could manage the horses on her own. She just waved her father out of the room with the words, "I'll ask her."

Stefan looked satisfied, and Sofie *felt* satisfied with her innocent lie.

"Now I have to sleep," she said with a great yawn.

"Sure. Good night. I'll try to make it over to the orthopedic clinic tomorrow and say hi to George. I'm sure he knows somebody…"

"Mm," Sofie mumbled, almost in her sleep.

She was pretty sure that George didn't have any acquaintances that could take care of his horses, because if that were case they would have been doing it already. But that was something she'd have to worry about another day.

87

A Small Revenge

Monday morning was chaotic. For the first time in years, the entire family got up early and had different places to go.

Sofie was the first to get up, because she had to head over to Lisa and Mrs. Brown. As she had the day before, Lisa stood just inside the gate, not budging an inch. But unlike last time, Sofie didn't hesitate. She walked straight into the paddock and carefully, but very decisively, pushed the little mare away by leaning against her shoulder.

Sofie placed the buckets where Mrs. Brown couldn't reach them and managed to pour the fodder into the feeder before the hungry horse started eating.

When she scattered the hay, the pheasant cock came strutting over. He screamed loudly and Sofie wondered if this was his way of thanking her for his food – or of telling her he was dissatisfied with something.

The morning was windy with a drizzle, and Sofie was very satisfied with herself when she remembered to put rain sheets on the horses. She took the fly-blankets off and placed them on the shelf in the stable.

"This afternoon, I'm going to groom you and make you beautiful!" she told them when she carefully closed the gate to the paddock. She knew that it wasn't necessary to groom them, but she wanted to care a little extra for George's horses.

In spite of the early morning, Sofie felt happy when she sneaked onto the porch and hung her stable clothes on their hook. She could manage this! It felt unnecessary to find somebody else, now that everything was working out so well.

Two minutes later, she wasn't too sure of that anymore, partly because it was way too late and partly because of the total chaos in her home. Somehow, Sofie had expected to find breakfast on the table when she came back from their neighbor's stable. Instead, she found her mother in front of the mirror in the hall, dressed only in underwear and noticeably nervous for her first day at work.

"I don't know what to wear!" Elizabeth moaned, holding up two different tops in front of her.

"The one with the flowery pattern," Sofie suggested as she ran past.

"You think so?" Elizabeth held it up in front of her and scrutinized her mirror image. "Don't I look too old in it?"

"But you are old." Sofie was halfway to the fridge, looking for something to eat.

"So I'll wear the white one," her mother replied, running upstairs to find a matching skirt – or maybe a pair of pants.

Of course, Sofie had forgotten to pack her backpack the night before and had to run around the house with a sandwich in one hand while she tried to collect everything for her gym bag.

"Where are my shorts?" she called from upstairs.

"What shorts?" her mother replied downstairs.

"The ones I use in gym class!"

"Which ones are those?"

Sofie sighed.

"Forget it!" She found a couple of old cotton shorts in a drawer and threw them into the bag with the rest of her stuff.

In the shower, she realized that she actually had had some homework over the weekend. She was supposed to have written down a favorite recipe for home economics. Sofie stomped the tiled floor. Typical! There was no way she would have time to write down a recipe now. The bus would be there in ten minutes.

❀ ❀ ❀ ❀

At seven fifteen, Sofie thudded down on a seat in the back of the school bus. Her hair was still wet, and she was sweaty and felt discombobulated. Had she remembered everything? She felt in her backpack. Well, everything except that recipe anyway…

When she turned to answer something that Jack was saying, she saw *him* out of the corner of her eye.

Adam.

On a seat in the row behind her, he was sitting looking out the window. He wore a denim jacket, and under that she caught a glimpse of a green T-shirt that matched his eyes. Sofie could feel a tingling in her stomach. The weekend had rushed by so quickly, and after George's accident, she had actually never thought about Adam.

She listened to Jack without really hearing what he said while she carefully studied Adam's profile. Every now and then she nodded, so that it wouldn't look strange that she was turned the wrong way.

Adam seemed completely focused on whatever was outside the window. She wondered what he was thinking about.

"Do you want to?" Jack called out after a while. "That's great!"

Sofie awoke from her dreams and looked at Jack.
"Want to what?"
Jack looked confused.
"You just said that you'd go with me to see that new robot movie."
"I did?"
Jack studied Sofie's face.
"You nodded. That means yes."
"I'm sorry, Jack, but I was thinking about something else. I actually *can't* go to the movies."
"Why not?"
"I'm taking care of George's horses. He's broken his leg."
Sofie knew that Jack often talked to George. Lisa and

Mrs. Brown's paddock stretched past both the Lindquists' house and the neighbors' garden. Jack liked to feed the horses and knew them well.

"Mom told me." At first Jack looked disappointed, but then he brightened. "But later? When George's leg is all right! Then we can see the movie."

"George won't be able to take care of his horses for a long time," Sofie said, relating what her dad had said the night before. "I guess the film won't be on anymore by then. Ask somebody in your class instead," she suggested.

"Okay."

The bus stopped and Adam's friends poured in. Sofie thought that Isabelle probably had been right when she guessed that Adam had had a sleepover at some friend's place. She sat up straight in her seat and turned toward the front. It would be extremely embarrassing if one of the boys saw her looking at them.

❀ ❀ ❀ ❀

Sofie had hardly gotten off the bus before she was attacked by Nathalie and her two clones. Her stomach tightened. She hadn't had any time to think about Adam, and the same was true of Nathalie. Now she was reminded of the girl in an unpleasant way.

"Hiii!" Nathalie smiled a fake smile. "Was your weekend nice?"

"Very," Sofie said quietly, wondering what Nathalie was getting at. She knew very well that the blonde girl didn't give a fig about what she had been doing.

"We've had a great time anyway!" Nathalie bubbled, turning to Fanny and Camilla for support. "Haven't we, girls?"

The two girls nodded and giggled.

"That's good," Sofie muttered, starting to walk toward the school.

Nathalie followed her.

"We were at a party! At Adam's place. He's in ninth grade. There were lots of people there and we danced half the night."

Sofie went cold inside. Adam's place? *Her* Adam? Did Nathalie know Adam Kempf?

"They have such a great house," Nathalie went on. "It's like a real mansion. And they have a pool… It's a pity you weren't invited."

Nathalie didn't look very sad when she said that.

"They're very rich, you know, Adam's family," she went on. "You know, his dad owns a lot of trotting horses and so on. But Adam isn't stuck up anyway, not at all. He doesn't brag about it like certain other upper class kids…"

Sofie could feel her anger welling up all the way from her toes. It stampeded through her stomach and continued up to her head.

But she kept her poise. Instead, she just said, "By the way, Isabelle Sandberg said hi to you."

Nathalie stopped and stared at Sofie.

"D-do you know Isabelle?" At once, all her cockiness was gone. Sofie could clearly see that the blonde girl made an effort to look cool, but her reaction was unmistakable. She actually looked scared.

"We're cousins," Sofie said. She shouldered past the three girls and walked quickly up the stairs to the school door.

When she was inside, out of earshot from her pursuers, she couldn't help quietly saying to herself, "Yes!"

Her line about Isabelle had worked perfectly. And Sofie was sure that Nathalie would stop bullying her now.

It wasn't really nice to use people's weaknesses or

93

fears to get at them, but Sofie thought that Nathalie was more than deserving of a counterattack, even using shady methods. Nathalie had more or less asked for it.

Isabelle had told Sofie that Nathalie's dad, John, owned a small accounting firm. He specialized in keeping books for horse owners and one of his biggest customers was Humleby Farm.

A few years ago, Sofie's uncle had discovered that Nathalie's dad had transferred a very large sum of money from Humleby Farm to his own firm. Tommy Sandberg had immediately gone to face John Almgren.

Nathalie's dad had admitted to embezzlement and begged on his knees for Tommy to not go to the police. He had explained that he had had trouble with his finances and that he had panicked. It would never happen again.

Tommy never did go to the police, but the rumor of the embezzlement had circulated in a few weeks and many of John's customers went to other firms. This meant that as a result of his illegal transfer, Nathalie's dad got into even worse trouble.

After being persuaded by Maggie, Tommy decided to let Humleby Farm stay with the Almgren accounting firm, and Nathalie's dad knew very well that his company had survived thanks to Tommy.

This meant that John Almgren owed the Sandbergs quite a lot – and Nathalie knew this. No doubt she also knew that her dad was dependent on having Humleby Farm as a customer.

"Mom felt bad about Nathalie and her siblings," Isabelle had explained when Sofie asked why Maggie had defended John Almgren. "Nathalie's mom was out of work at the time, and if their firm had gone bankrupt, they would have been in serious trouble."

"But what he did was illegal!" Sofie had protested, feeling enraged.

Isabelle had shrugged her shoulders.

"Mom thought that Nathalie's dad was punished enough when his customers left him. He had to live with the shame."

"So why did he have money troubles to begin with?" Sofie was curious about Nathalie's family, and it was obvious that Nathalie had found out that Sofie's dad was a doctor – which meant that Sofie felt entitled to do some snooping of her own.

Isabelle had shrugged again.

"I don't know," she had said. "He probably had a bad night at Jägersro. We heard that he gambled on horses, Nathalie's dad. And I think he sometimes gambles with more money than he has."

Sofie had decided not to use the information from Isabelle if she didn't have to. Somehow she had hoped that Nathalie would be a changed person on Monday morning, that she would have realized her mistake. She guessed that Nathalie probably wouldn't apologize, but hoped that at least she would leave Sofie alone.

But the attack a few minutes ago showed that Nathalie was the same person she had been on Friday, and Sofie didn't feel bad about what she had said. She hoped that Nathalie would leave her alone now.

The only thing bothering Sofie was the party that Nathalie had mentioned. That it had been at Adam Kempf's house was obvious, and Sofie couldn't help wondering how close Nathalie and Adam were. He looked so nice. Could he really like somebody like Nathalie?

Sofie went to her locker and opened it. On her way there, she nodded at the guy who had comforted her at the English class on Friday. He smiled and nodded back.

The worry in her stomach eased a little. Maybe she would find a few friends at this school after all. After all, this was only her third day.

But when she closed the locker and turned around to go to the home economics class, she saw that a whole flock of girls had gathered around Nathalie. Everybody was glaring angrily at Sofie when she passed, and all her hopes disappeared as quickly as they had formed.

Good Advice

When Sofie opened her inbox on Monday night, for the first time in days, she found three messages from Jojo. The first one was titled "How are you?", the second one "Where are you?", and the third one "Hellooooo!"

> From: Sofie Lindquist <sofiesofine@swede-mail.com>
> Date: Monday, August 26, 2009, 20:07
> To: Joanna Nilsson <jojo_sweetie@britmail.com>
> Subject: Re: Hellooooo!

Hi Jo,

I'm sorry about not answering, but a lot of things have happened this weekend. I'm taking care of George's horses (the two that hang out in the paddock next door), since he broke his leg. This means I have to get up at five every morning... And so on.

Since you seem to long for a new school and more excitement in your life, I have a nice offer: You can have my life if I can have yours.

I think you won't mind staying in London when you've read the latest news:

1. Nathalie still hates me, and although I really put her in place today, she keeps being mean. Now she's managed to get every girl in class on her side. Nobody talks to me. I hate school!

2. Every teacher keeps going on about the fact that I've lived in England. In home economics, this embarrassing woman thought I should bring a recipe for steak and kidney pie. Everybody in the class looked like they wanted to puke, but the teacher just laughed and said that offal is good food.

3. Speedy's having an operation! They found nothing in the X-rays, and now they're opening his knee to have a look. I don't really know how this is done, but I understand that Speedy probably won't be able to race all fall. What if this means that Axel wants to sell him?

4. George's horses are weird. Lisa is acting like she wants to eat me alive. She's never been like this before!

5. Mom and Dad keep nagging me about finding somebody else to take care of Lisa and Mrs. Brown. I've told them that they have to do that themselves, since I don't have the time.

6. I'm so tired I have double vision.

Miss you lots!
Sofie

It seemed like Jojo had been waiting at her computer, because as Sofie wrote a short message to Emma, her e-mail program beeped.

From: Joanna Nilsson < jojo_sweetie@britmail.com>
Date: Thursday, August 22, 2009, 17:16
To: Joanna Nilsson <sofiesofine@swede-mail.com>
Subject: Re: Re: Hellooooo!

Hi Sofie!

Wow, talk about action – your life would make a great movie! (Sorry, I couldn't help myself…)

I <u>understand</u> that you're having a hard time in school and I'm really, really sorry for you. But maybe I, sitting here at the other side of the North Sea some distance from your life, can give you a few little suggestions:

1. Never mind Nathalie. I still think there has to be at least <u>one</u> sensible person in your class.

2. Bring your mom's recipe for mincemeat pie – the one without offal but with feta cheese! If you make that, the entire class will drop their chins in awe!

3. Speedy's going to get well. And why would Axel want to sell a horse that just won a big race? Last time you wrote that Tina wasn't worried.

4. Ask Isabelle for help. (Note – this will also solve problems five and six.)

Good luck!

Hugs,
Jojo

At first, Sofie felt angry when she read Jojo's answer. "Never mind Nathalie…" It sounded as if Jojo thought that you could make Nathalie disappear by just pushing a button. Sofie thought that Jojo was playing down her problems. She had wanted compassion and just got some brisk advice.

But then she read the e-mail again and thought that Jojo might be right – at least about a few things.

For instance, it was probable that Speedy would get well. Nobody had hinted at anything else. Tommy's worried look probably was due to his having such great expectations for the new star of the stable. If things worked out for the best, it just meant that his expectations would be slightly delayed.

Also, Sofie realized that she had to swallow her pride and ask Isabelle for help with Lisa and Mrs. Brown.

First of all, she was tired of her parents' nagging. Secondly, she was tired in every conceivable way – actually more like half dead. And thirdly Jimmy, her homeroom teacher, had told them that there would be a field day next week. Sofie had wanted to try athletics, but when it was her turn to sign the list, that group was already full. That meant she had to choose between canoeing and ball games. She chose canoeing when, at the last moment, she saw Nathalie's name under the heading *Ball Games*.

The canoeing trip would take place at a lake many miles inland, which meant that she wouldn't be home until late in the evening. That was a day when she really would need help with George's horses. And she very much doubted that any other help would turn up before then.

❊ ❊ ❊ ❊

On Tuesday afternoon, Sofie quickly walked over to Humleby Farm. She hoped that Isabelle would be home. It felt strange to have to unlock the door when she came home from school. She was so used to being met by an open door and a mom with lots of questions.

On the bus ride home, Sofie had more or less been planning to tell Elizabeth about Nathalie. She felt a great need to get this burden off her chest, and at least her mom was usually a good listener.

Sofie often felt that Elizabeth overreacted to things, and her mom also had a tendency to ask interminable questions. But this afternoon Sofie would have gladly overlooked her mother's faults just for the chance to spill some of her sorrow and frustration.

Sofie almost cried when she got home and realized that Elizabeth was still at work. She had totally forgotten that her mom was now a professional woman, and the house seemed eerily silent and empty when she walked in.

I guess that's how it is to have a working mom! Sofie thought angrily as she threw her backpack in the hall. *I'm sure she'll never ever have time for me again!*

When she closed the door and locked it, she decided that was just as well. She would manage on her own! There was really no use dragging Elizabeth into this – she would probably just mess things up even more.

It was a nice, sunny day. Sofie drew a deep breath, as if to clean her lungs from the stale school air. The smell of ripe apples still hung over Humleby. The other day, Jack's mom had said that this was an apple year, and by now most gardens had drifts of windfalls that nobody – except for the wasps and pheasants – bothered to take care of. Of course, horses also liked apples, but they couldn't eat too many or they'd get stomachaches.

❀ ❀ ❀ ❀

Sofie walked through the open gate and across the yard. She waved to Roger, the farrier and jack-of-all trades at the farm, as he walked out of the lower stable with a chocolate-brown gelding named Cookie. Well, the horse was actually named Chocolate Chip Cookie, but nobody bothered to call him that.

Sofie still thought it strange that horses had to have such long and cumbersome names, but in the next moment, she thought that maybe it wasn't that strange after all. She herself was named Anna Sofie Elizabeth Lindquist, but people just called her Sofie. That was almost the same thing.

She moved to the side to allow for a big truck, heading

out for the village road. The driver raised his hand to thank her and Sofie nodded. She recognized him. It was the guy who picked up the manure from the farm and left an empty container in its place.

Tommy had explained that Humleby Farm, with its exceptionally high number of animals, couldn't possibly make do with just an ordinary dung heap behind the stables. It would grow to be a small mountain in just a few days.

Sofie walked toward the little stable. She couldn't very well pass Speedy without saying hello.

Tina was crouched in the passageway. She whistled quietly as she painted Tornado's hooves with something. The black horse's eyes met Sofie's.

"Hi there!" Sofie put her hand out and let him smell it. Then she stroked the soft bridge of the gelding's nose. "You're beautiful, do you know that?" she said, looking into his dark eyes.

Tina looked up.

"Oh, we have a prominent guest!" She put the lid on the jar of hoof grease and stood. "How's everything?"

"Well…" Sofie wasn't sure if she could bear telling the truth. She was afraid that she'd start crying if she said anything about the school. "So-so," she said evasively. "How's Speedy?"

Tina gave Sofie a penetrating look but didn't say anything. Instead, she turned and looked at the chestnut's box.

"Well, I can't really say he's fine, since he isn't…" Sofie sighed.

"But…" Tina went on, "I'm sure he'll get well in time. We just have to be patient."

Patience wasn't Sofie's forte.

102

"Do you think Axel's going to sell him now?" she asked uncertainly.

Tina smiled.

"Not because of his knee… Not after his great race last Tuesday. I just can't imagine that." Then she looked a little more serious. "But *all* the horses here can be sold and moved out at anytime, you know that."

Sofie nodded. She hated it that Speedy was owned by a man she hadn't met and didn't know anything about. She wanted Speedy to stay at Humleby Farm forever.

A while ago, one of the mares in the upper stable had been sold and moved to Denmark. Sofie hadn't known the horse very well, but she dreaded the day when she would have to say goodbye to one of her favorites. She knew that the day would come sooner or later.

Sofie walked over to Speedy's box. His head was out in the passageway, and when he saw her he threw it back and forth until his blond mane flew.

"Don't take it personally," Tina said, laughing. "He's bored." She called to Speedy, "Stop that immediately!"

And to Sofie's great surprise, the horse calmed right down.

Sofie caressed the chestnut's neck.

"When's his operation?" she asked Tina, as she changed spots and started scratching Speedy between his ears.

Tina walked up to them.

"On Thursday," she said, giving her protégé a little pat. "We were lucky to get scheduled that soon. Weren't we? What do you say, Speedy?"

Speedy neighed softly and Sofie smiled. It was just as if the two could talk to each other.

"The woman who whispered to horses," she said, thinking about a book on Isabelle's shelf, *The Horse Whisperer*.

Tina laughed.

"How long will he have to rest afterwards?" Sofie asked.

"That depends a little on what they find in his knee, but if his lameness is due to wear, he probably won't be able to race until February."

Sofie's eyes widened.

"Will he have to stay in his box until then? He'll go crazy!"

"No, he won't be in his box for six months – I was just talking about when he'll be able to race again."

Tina put the jar of hoof grease among the other grooming things and went on, "My bet is he'll have to rest completely for a month. Then we'll train him more and more as time goes by."

"A month is a long time…" Sofie thought for a while. "What if he gets nervous and weird, like he was when he came here?"

"Horses are very adaptable," Tina said. "And if you're worried that you won't be able to cope with him, I think that's unnecessary." She smiled. "Don't forget that you were a complete rookie when Speedy came here."

"That's right."

"I'm sure our favorite guy will be a little bored at first…" Tina stoked Speedy's neck with her hand, "but you and Isabelle can take turns entertaining him in the afternoons!" she laughed.

This comment reminded Sofie of why she was there.

"I'll be back," she said. "I'll just check to see if Isabelle's home."

"Okay." Tina moved a wheelbarrow with old sawdust, allowing her to open the door to Tornado's box. Sofie squeezed past the black gelding and walked out in the yard.

I have to be a little smart when I ask her, she thought as she waved to Ewa, one of the horse minders. Sofie was worried that if Isabelle didn't want to help her with Lisa and Mrs. Brown, her parents would make sure that the two horses were moved to another stable very soon.

She just couldn't let that happen. Sofie wanted George to be able to see his horses as soon as he was well enough. If they weren't there, she would have broken her promise to him.

A Brown Thief

"You're right!" Isabelle mildly but decisively pushed Lisa away, so that the two girls could get into the paddock. "She's really weird!"

Lisa neighed shrilly, as if she wanted to deny what Isabelle had said.

"I don't know what's gotten into her," Sofie complained. "She's been like this since Sunday. Saturday was no problem at all… but then…"

Lisa snapped at the fodder buckets.

"You think she's sick?" Sofie couldn't help but worrying.

"No," Isabelle said, immediately walking toward Lisa's feeder and closely followed by the little mare. "She looks quite well."

Sofie raked up old hay from the side of the paddock and scattered new while Isabelle walked over to Mrs. Brown's feeder and emptied the other white bucket there. Mrs. Brown watched curiously as Sofie worked. The mare pushed a little at the rake.

"Get out of here!" Sofie laughed. "Go eat your supper instead."

Isabelle walked up to Sofie with the two empty buckets dangling from her right hand.

106

"I don't think Lisa's sick. I think she's hungry. Are you sure you've fed her every day?"

"Of course I'm sure!"

Stupid question, Sofie thought. But in the next moment, both she and Isabelle saw Mrs. Brown heading for Lisa's feeder and pushing her buddy away from her food. Lisa protested wildly but didn't stand a chance against the bigger, heavier horse. Mrs. Brown quickly wolfed down everything in the feeder and then walked over to her own.

"There's your explanation," Isabelle said. "No wonder Lisa's been wanting to eat you alive. I don't think she's had very much food these last few days."

"Oh, no!" Sofie felt a cold sweat breaking out. "What should I do?"

"Get more food," Isabelle simply said. "And tie Mrs. Brown up to her feeder while Lisa eats."

Of course. Sofie was so ashamed that her earlobes felt hot.

How had she managed to miss Mrs. Brown stealing the food? What if Lisa was close to dying from starvation? Panic was closing in. She had managed to starve a horse for four days! Would Lisa suffer permanent injuries?

"I can't understand how this could happen! I've been here all the time!" Sofie was desperate.

"Haven't you been going for hay after giving them their fodder?"

Sofie thought.

"Yes… but…"

"Then it's no wonder you didn't notice, right?" Isabelle looked intently at her younger cousin. "Come on, Sofie! It's not the end of the world! I'm sure Lisa's gotten a little food every day – at least she's had hay to chew on. Now go get a little more oats, and I'll tie the glutton up."

Isabelle's words got Sofie going. She ran out of the paddock, across the road and into the stable. To compensate Lisa, she poured an extra big meal and hurried back.

❀ ❀ ❀ ❀

"It's a good thing that you came along." The girls were sitting in the grass not far from Lisa, who was now eating ravenously. "What if this had gone on for weeks? Poor Lisa!"

Sofie still felt ashamed.

Isabelle smiled.

"I'm sure you'd have noticed sooner or later."

"Maybe…" Sofie turned to her cousin. "Thanks for agreeing to help me next week. You're really great."

"No problem," Isabelle said. "I scratch your back, you scratch mine, you know…" She grinned.

"Of course! Just tell me what to do."

Isabelle pushed Sofie.

"Never mind," she said. "Of course we have to help each other! We're cousins and all, right?"

Sofie smiled gratefully at Isabelle.

It hadn't been quite that easy to get Isabelle to help with George's horses.

"What if somebody sees me!" she had said. "I don't want to be seen among those amateurs!"

But Sofie had mollified her by saying that it might be a *good* thing for a pro to come to the stable – maybe the amateurs could learn a few things.

And as soon as Isabelle had said hello to Lisa and Mrs. Brown, she had taken to the two pretty mares, just like Sofie, and offered to do the evening chores for a week.

Sofie knew that Isabelle was a great animal lover, and she also knew that her cousin was empathetic enough to George's situation.

This meant that this week was arranged, but the problem wasn't entirely solved. Isabelle would be starting her practical training in two weeks, and that would leave her no time for anything but school, training and Humleby Farm.

One week, Sofie had thought. Maybe her parents would manage to put an ad in the paper during that time? She thought that there had to be lots of horse-crazy girls who would like to take care of Lisa and Mrs. Brown – at least during the weekends.

That would mean that George's horses could stay in their paddock and that Sofie could still be mainly

109

responsible for them. Now, when she knew that she had
to tie Mrs. Brown up at feeding time, she was sure there
wouldn't be any more problems with getting in and out of
the paddock. Lisa would probably calm down.

❀ ❀ ❀ ❀

"So how was school today?" Isabelle's question made Sofie
return to reality. With a sigh, she lay down on her back in
the grass, studying a couple of small fluffy clouds in the
otherwise clear blue sky.

"Actually, not very good." Sofie told her cousin how
Nathalie had made all the girls in the class glare angrily at
her.

Isabelle's eyes flashed.

"That girl's not right in her head! She *knows* that if we
end our contract with Almgren's Accountants, her dad will
be out of a job!" She looked into Sofie's eyes. "Do you
want me to talk to Mom and Dad?"

Sofie pondered for a moment. The thought actually
was quite tempting, but she said, "No, I don't think so. It
wouldn't feel fair."

Isabelle yanked up a fistful of grass and threw it at her
cousin.

"Why should you be fair to her? She's acting like an
idiot!"

More blades of grass flew in the same direction.

"If her dad loses his job, it won't hurt just Nathalie,"
Sofie explained. "It'll hurt her entire family."

"Let 'em have it!" Isabelle said.

Sofie often felt that her cousin seemed to like animals
better than people. Today there definitely seemed to be
some truth to this thought.

"One of the guys in class said that Nathalie's bound to
stop bullying me after a while. He said she usually does…"

Sofie didn't know why she was defending her classmate, when she actually thought it was unbearable to be in school, to have to stand all the mean comments and glances.

"All right…" Isabelle sighed. "I give up. But tell me if you need help. I hate that snobby girl, and I wouldn't mind at all if I could get at her."

"Promise." Sofie almost laughed when she thought about the fact that just a couple of months ago, she had thought that *Isabelle* was the most snobbish, meanest girl she had ever met. "Thanks!"

"Not at all." Isabelle stood. "Well, I have to go home and start my homework now. Just don't forget to let Mrs. Brown loose before you leave."

"I'll do it right now." Sofie jumped to her feet. "Lisa's done eating now."

Isabelle walked two steps and then turned around.

"Hey, by the way…" She smiled impishly. "How are things with Adam?"

Sofie's face was hot.

"Fine… or well, so-so…" She nervously twisted a strand of hair around her finger. "He's on the bus."

"Talk to him!" Isabelle said cheerily. "He's nice."

"Maybe."

Sofie knew that this was something that would *never* happen. Never, ever. To walk up to a strange boy was the last thing she'd do. Especially now, when she knew that he was friends with Nathalie and her buddies.

Sofie could hardly imagine what would happen if she were brave enough to talk to him. Adam would probably just stare at her. Or laugh.

"See you!" Isabelle called when she closed the gate to the paddock. "I'll take care of the horses tomorrow night."

"Great!" Sofie gave her a thumbs-up and went to release Mrs. Brown. As she worked, she thought about Adam's beautiful eyes.

And strangely enough, she felt almost a little elated – in spite of everything that was troubling her.

In the saddle at last

After living through an entire week of cold glances and mean comments, Saturday felt like a relief.

It was late afternoon and Sofie was done with the day's chores. She sat with her back against Speedy's box and watched her older cousin groom Rocky. The stallion had had an easy workout at the track with a few of the other horses and was now newly showered and dried and tied up in the passageway.

"I can't understand how you can stand school!" Isabelle combed through Rocky's tail one last time and then moved to his mane.

"Me neither," Sofie said. "I get stomach pains just thinking that it'll soon be Monday again."

"Have you said anything to your parents?"

Sofie drew her legs up, hugging them with her arms.

"No…" She put her chin on her knees, making it press against them when she talked. "Mom understands that I'm not very happy there, but I know that if she learned that Nathalie is being mean, she'd call her parents immediately – or the headmaster. And that would only make everything worse… Dad thinks everything's hunky dory. He's mostly been bugging me about how George's horses steal time from my schoolwork."

"But you have to tell them if it doesn't get better. You can't live like this!"

Isabelle felt sorry for Sofie. Maybe they hadn't really liked each other in the beginning – mainly because she herself had acted badly – but Isabelle had started appreciating having a girlfriend in the village. Sofie was fun and smart, even though she was only thirteen. That she had become interested in horses was another plus.

Isabelle felt ashamed when she thought about how she, early in the summer, had made fun of her younger cousin for not knowing anything about horses. It must have been so hard for Sofie to move away from her best friend – and be met by a sour, disagreeable cousin.

Isabelle had asked forgiveness several times, and Sofie didn't seem to carry a grudge. This felt good, but now Isabelle was suffering on Sofie's behalf now that Sofie, yet again, had to deal with a disagreeable girl. She wished that there was something she could do, but she didn't know what.

"I know…" Sofie stretched her legs again. "Actually, I have so much to do that I hardly have had time to feel bad. At night I fall asleep immediately – I don't have to think about school. Working with horses is a good way to escape your problems…"

"You've run into bad luck." Isabelle stopped working and looked at her younger cousin with compassion. "It could have been the other way around. You could have gotten into a great class, with no Nathalies."

Sofie nodded.

"I know. It feels so unfair. The alternatives seem much better than the reality. All of them."

"It's Nathalie's fault," Isabelle felt.

"Yeah…" Sofie was quiet for a while. "But," she went

114

on, "the other girls add to it. They just do whatever she tells them."

Isabelle scrutinized the dark-brown stallion and seemed satisfied with what she saw. She turned to her cousin again.

"Actually, you're right," she said, unleashing Rocky. "I haven't thought about the fact that the hangers-on are as bad as the bullies."

"Me neither," Sofie admitted. "Not until now." She stood and looked at the lame horse in the box behind her. "Speedy seems tired," she said.

Isabelle led Rocky into his box and then came up to Sofie.

"Yes, he does seem a little tired after his operation… but he'll get better."

As if he had heard her last comment, Speedy came up to the opening in the bars and put his head out in the passageway.

"Hi, favorite!" Sofie caressed his velvety muzzle. "How are you doing?"

The gelding snorted air onto Sofie's hand and she smiled.

"You'll soon be back on track again, literally," she said encouragingly. "And then you'll be better than ever!"

Just as Tina and Tommy had suspected, Speedy's lameness was due to wear in his knee joint. According to Andersson, the operation had gone perfectly; he had cleaned up the joint, and now it looked great. But as Tina had guessed, the operation meant that Speedy wouldn't be ready to race until late February.

The gelding had been sedated and then kept under observation for a day and a night. Everything had gone according to plan, and on Friday afternoon Speedy had been back at Humleby Farm again.

The clinic was close to the home track, which was good for everybody involved.

"Well, I'm sure he won't be worse than before, anyway," Isabelle chimed in. "What are we going to do now?" she said. "We can't really walk over to Lisa and Mrs. Brown just yet."

Sofie shrugged. She was tired – as usual – but she didn't feel like sleeping away a free afternoon. Then she saw Jenny out in the yard and had an idea.

"You want to ride?"

Isabelle's eyes widened in surprise.

"You've never ridden, have you?"

"No, but there's a first time for everything, right?" Sofie said cheerily.

Isabelle stared at her younger cousin, somewhat skeptically.

"Don't look like that!" Sofie exclaimed. "Jenny actually has *said* that she'll let me ride some day."

Isabelle smiled.

"All right! Why not? It's been a long time since I was on horseback myself, so it might be fun."

"Come on!" Sofie felt more enthusiastic than she had in a long time. "Let's run after Jenny and ask her which horses we can use!"

Isabelle giggled. "Too bad we don't have a pony for you. Or some tired old Icelandic horse."

"Why's that?" Sofie protested boldly. "If I can just ride a horse that's calm and sweet, everything'll work out just fine."

❋ ❋ ❋ ❋

"That's better! Now put your other foot in the stirrup and hold the reins."

"Where's the backrest?" Sofie was beginning to fear

she had made a mistake. "It feels like the ground's a mile away."

"Ha, ha!" Jenny laughed heartily. "You remember now what I said before?"

"No, what did you say?" Sofie reeled as Sky stepped to the side, but she managed to find her balance again.

"Help, what's he doing?"

"He's just impatient," Isabelle explained.

They had decided to take a short trip to an empty paddock close to the stable. Jenny would lead Sky with Sofie in the saddle and Isabelle would ride Oh My Glory.

"Now, take a deep breath and try to remember what to do to make him walk." Jenny smiled at Sofie, who looked pale. "Keep your back straight!" the older girl with reddish-blonde hair reminded her, and Sofie cautiously straightened up.

Jenny had given Sofie a short tutorial before she was allowed to mount. Jenny told her it was against every rule not to teach Sofie better before letting her ride, but she had promised to hold Sky steadily.

If Sofie liked riding today, she would get a real lesson some other day.

Sofie felt very small sitting on Sky, who in spite of his name – Little Skywalker – was an unusually big gelding. She cautiously pressed her legs against the horse's sides and smacked her lips.

What a feeling it was when the horse started moving in the right direction! She smiled and forgot her fear for a moment.

"Good!" Jenny looked satisfied. "We'll turn to the right in a moment," she went on. "Sky knows where to go, but why don't you just help him a little. Use the reins."

Walking slowly, they passed the barrack and the first paddock, where Lady and Star were grazing. Sofie relaxed

117

more and more. Sky was cool as a cucumber and didn't seem to feel that his rider was uncertain. When they arrived at the paddock, Sofie even dared to lean forwards and pat the dark-brown horse on his neck.

"You're a nice guy, Sky," she whispered with her nose in his black mane.

❀ ❀ ❀ ❀

Her ride ended all too soon. After walking around the paddock three times, they turned back to the stable again. Jenny was finished for the day and had to go somewhere.

Sofie could have gone on forever – riding had been unbelievably fun. A little scary, but fun. Riding was something she definitely wanted to try again!

"Just tell me when you need help!" Sofie said to Jenny as she slid off Sky's back and landed with both feet on the ground again.

"Absolutely!" Jenny laughed. "It feels good to have a stand-in!"

"But what about me? I want to ride, too!" Isabelle dismounted and patted Oh My Glory, who seemed disappointed that it was over so soon. He neighed loudly and stomped in place.

"I think there's room for everybody." Jenny smiled. "There are forty horses here, and almost all of them need to be ridden once in a while. And also, Sofie needs a couple more lessons before we let her out on her own, right?"

"Just kidding," Isabelle said, unbuckling her riding helmet. "Of course there's room!"

Sofie was wild with enthusiasm.

"Imagine, when I've practiced a little more – we can ride out together!" In her imagination, she saw herself sitting on Speedy's back, wind in her face and hair fluttering behind her back.

Isabelle nodded.

"Maybe you'd like to try driving sometime, too? It's really fun!"

"Riding seems more fun," Sofie protested.

"You don't know until you've tried! I promise you, it's a great feeling when you're sitting in the sulky behind a real fast horse."

"I believe you," Sofie said, "and I also think that I can manage without that feeling for a while."

Jenny laughed. "You mean, one thing at a time?"

"Right." Sofie smiled and turned to Isabelle. "Will you come with me to see Lisa and Mrs. Brown when we're done with these guys?"

"Yes, you can show me where everything is." Isabelle turned Oh My Glory around to lead him into the stable. "I might as well prepare to do the evenings next week."

"That's great!"

Zoe

No Adam, Sofie noted with disappointment, sinking into a seat in the middle of the school bus.

It was Monday morning, and Sofie was tired. Tired in body and soul. She sent Isabelle a grateful thought: It was so great that she wouldn't have to feed Lisa and Mrs. Brown this week.

On Sunday night Sofie had had to admit – both to herself and to her parents – that she couldn't really manage George's horses on her own. She had had a hard time coming to this conclusion, but unfortunately it was true.

First of all, it took a lot of time to take care of two horses morning and evening. And doing the same job during the weekends, when she also had her job at Humleby Farm all day, was exhausting. She'd had neither the time nor the stamina to do any homework at all in the week that had passed.

Secondly, the work was heavy. The hay had to be brought down from the loft and then put in the wheelbarrow and driven out. Old hay and manure had to be raked up and driven in the other direction. The sacks of oats were heavy and the faucet for the horses' water seemed to be stuck somehow – she always worked herself into a sweat trying to open it.

121

But the physical part of the work wasn't the worst. The worst was the responsibility.

At first, she hadn't thought about that at all. She had just thought it was an exciting challenge to take care of two horses all by herself.

But when Isabelle discovered that Mrs. Brown had been stealing Lisa's food for four days, Sofie had suddenly realized that the lives of two living creatures were in her hands. It was *her* responsibility to see to it that nothing happened to the two mares. And that had made her nervous – and her nervousness had become worse with each passing day.

George trusted that his horses were fine. Thomas trusted that the horses at his stable were well taken care of. George was ill, and everybody else had so much to do that nobody really had the time to care how she was actually doing. It was true that Thomas had come out to the stable one evening to ask her if she had enough oats, but he hadn't asked if she needed any help. Sofie got the feeling that he'd hurried away, worried that Sofie might ask for something that would take up too much of his time.

George had also been in touch. He had called from his hospital bed on Sunday morning, asking how his horses were. Sofie thought that he sounded so weak that she immediately assured him that everything was fine and dandy. She hadn't said a single word about being worried that she might not be up to the task.

Because of this, Sofie was extra grateful that Isabelle was going to help with the horses this week. Isabelle had a trained eye and would notice if there was something wrong with them – and she usually knew how to solve problems. Sofie wouldn't have to worry that Isabelle would miss anything.

But a week would go by quickly. All too quickly.

The animated discussion on Sunday night – before Sofie admitted to not really being up to the task – had led to Sofie's parents making plans to move Lisa and Mrs. Brown to a stable a few miles south of Humleby. The stable was owned by a friend of Stefan's, a retired riding teacher who had promised to look out for the two mares as long as was needed. The horses were to move there in a week – when Sofie didn't have the time to help anymore.

Of course, the move was temporary, but still! Sofie didn't even want to think about having to tell George that the apples of his eye were going to move while he was bed-ridden.

She felt incredibly bad about not telling the old man the truth, but defended herself by thinking that she hadn't wanted to upset him when it wasn't necessary.

To somehow silence her conscience, Sofie had promised herself to do some more schoolwork. It didn't feel good to be lagging behind already, when it was only the second week.

"Are you sick or what?" Jack leaned across the aisle and poked Sofie's upper arm. Sofie, who had been sitting staring into space, jumped.

"What? Sick? No… Why?" She sounded more grumpy than she had intended.

"You look sick!" Jack said cheerily.

"Oh?" Sofie sighed. "Thank you."

Jack smiled, leaned back and started talking to a buddy in the seat next to him.

Two minutes later, the bus pulled up in front of the school and the students swarmed out. Sofie thought that if you could see this from above, it would look like a big, shiny monster spitting kids out onto the schoolyard.

And that was exactly how she felt. As if somebody, or something, had spit her out.

The schoolyard was bare and mostly covered with asphalt. There was nowhere to go if you didn't want to be seen. The corner with the Norway maple was the best place, since the branches of the tree hung down, offering protection, but it was still impossible to hide.

Sofie didn't even make it to the tree before she saw Nathalie, Fanny and Camilla. They came walking from the bicycle stands with firm steps, as if they had been waiting for her. Waiting for the opportunity of a new attack.

Sofie's heart sank in her chest. How long would they keep at it?

She wanted to turn around and run home. She wanted to call her mom or Isabelle. But it was too late. The three girls were already standing in front of her.

As usual, Nathalie spoke first. "Hi."

The word was clipped and she didn't even bother to smile.

"Hi." Sofie tried to keep her voice steady. She didn't want to show how unpleasant she thought this was.

Nathalie glared at her. "I hope you realize that it's *your* fault if my dad loses his contract with Humleby Farm now."

Sofie pretended not to understand. "What? What are you talking about?"

"I'm sure you know." Nathalie's eyes narrowed. "I'm sure your *cousin* told you." She made a face at the word "cousin."

"Isabelle just asked me to say hello to you," Sofie said as innocently as she could.

"And you want me to believe that?"

"You believe what you want." Sofie looked down. She hated lying and wasn't very good at it.

Once again, she was saved by the school bell, ringing

for the first class. She immediately started walking for the door. Nathalie didn't give up and followed close behind.

"You heard what I said!" she hissed in Sofie's ear. "It's *your* fault if something happens!"

Great, Sofie thought bleakly when she entered the school. So it's my fault if two horses are badly cared for or have to move, it's my fault if I fail in school and it's my fault if Nathalie's father loses his job and his family has to starve. I might as well take responsibility for global warming and all the wars going on in the world, too.

She hurried her steps and walked to her locker. Thankfully, Nathalie and her two cronies seemed to have given up for now. But there were only two classes before the morning break – and then they would probably begin again.

Sofie thought it was strange that nobody reacted to Nathalie's terror. Once or twice, she thought she had seen a glimpse of compassion in the eyes of other girls in the class. But it seemed nobody was strong enough to say anything.

What might happen, really, if somebody walked up to Nathalie and told her that she was mean and nasty and that she ought to stop bullying people? It was true that Nathalie was quite nasty, but Sofie didn't think she was capable of killing people.

Sighing, Sofie found her key and started opening the locker. She noted that keeping order in the small space was something else she hadn't taken care of. She ought to put protective paper or plastic on the books and get a pencil box. Maybe she would be able to make it into town on Friday afternoon? But she didn't really feel like it. As she rooted around for her math book, she was suddenly aware that somebody was standing behind her. Her stomach churned.

Could it be Nathalie, attacking once again? She slowly turned, expecting to look into a pair of icy blue eyes.

But she didn't. Right behind her was a girl with blonde, almost white, dreadlocks. A big black ribbon kept her hair away from heavily made up eyes. The girl was dressed in a short black skirt, thick black stockings with a hole on one knee and a black T-shirt. On her thin shoulders hung an angry-red vinyl-coated bag with a Hello Kitty logo.

"Hi," she said. "Are you in 7 C?"

"Yes… And you?"

"7 C."

"You are?" Sofie wondered how she had been able to miss this black-clad apparition for five days.

The girl put out her hand.

"Zoe," she said, smiling.

"What?"

"Zoe." The girl grinned. "Well, actually I'm named Sarah, but I think Zoe sounds cooler. What's your name?"

"Sofie." She couldn't stop staring at Zoe. The girl looked like something out of a music magazine or a teenage movie. "Are you sure you're in 7 C?" she said presently.

"Well, yeah, that was what the letter said, anyway."

"I haven't seen you."

Zoe smiled again.

"That would have been strange, since this is my first day. I wasn't here last week."

"So you're new in town too?" Sofie caught herself really hoping that Zoe would answer yes. That would mean that there were two of them.

"Yeah. We lived in Stockholm until Friday."

"Wow!" Sofie exclaimed. "Isn't moving a drag?" She realized exactly how terrible Zoe must think it had been.

The black-clad girl shrugged.

127

"Oh, I don't mind. I'm used to it."

Sofie stared at her without understanding.

"My dad's a minister, so we move pretty often," she explained, and Sofie stared even harder. Could you look like Zoe if your father was a minister? Weren't you supposed to look more pious? In her mind, a picture of a girl with braids, a lamb's-wool sweater and a pearl necklace quickly flashed by.

"Minister?"

"Yeah, a minister. You have any problem with ministers?" Zoe looked a little offended.

"Well, no…" Sofie could feel herself blushing. "Certainly not. I just… well…"

"You thought I don't look like a minister's daughter. Right?"

Sofie breathed out.

"Right." She smiled. "But I suppose you can look any way you want."

"Right on!" Zoe let out a ringing laugh that partly mixed with the second ring of the bell. "Can I tag along with you?" she asked.

"Sure! We're going that way." Sofie pointed to her right.

She couldn't help stealing a glance at the black-clad girl as they walked up the stairs. Zoe didn't seem worried at all. And she didn't seem to care about all the stares she attracted. Wasn't she nervous? In a minute, she would meet her new classmates for the first time.

But Zoe had said that she was used to it. And she seemed quite sure of herself.

Sofie envied her. Even Nathalie wouldn't dare try to get at somebody who radiated such confidence.

❁ ❁ ❁ ❁

It turned out Sofie was right. She spent the entire morning break showing Zoe the school and Nathalie seemed to be

128

hidden underground. Neither she, Fanny nor Camilla were to be seen anywhere.

Sofie had volunteered to take care of Zoe when Jimmy, in gym class after math, asked for somebody.

"Oh, you're already quite at home here!" the still quite tanned man said, smiling with all his white teeth. "That means Nathalie must have done a first-rate job."

Nathalie had smiled ingratiatingly at Jimmy and then glared hatefully in Sofie's direction.

"Wow!" Zoe had whispered. She and Sofie had been standing on the gravel lot behind the school "What a look! What have you done to her?

"Been alive," Sofie had said. "By the way, her name's Barbie, and the teacher's called Ken."

Zoe had shuddered with giggles and Sofie had joined in. It had felt wonderful.

"I see you two have already found each other." Jimmy looked satisfied, as if this was thanks to him. "Now let's play rounders! Stand in line and count one and two. Ones begin out and twos in, then we'll change places."

❀ ❀ ❀ ❀

Sofie and Zoe went together to the lunchroom. Sofie thought that if she had seen the black-clad girl in town, she would never have thought of her as somebody who could become a friend. Zoe was somebody that Sofie normally would have been very shy of. She looked so incredibly cool.

Sofie felt everything but cool. If everything had been as usual, Sofie would probably have thought that she looked like a gray mouse next to Zoe. But now here she was, walking along next to this black-clad and white-haired girl, feeling very comfortable with it.

Maybe she liked Zoe because Zoe was the first girl at school who had talked to her without being mean.

But on the other hand, it might be that Zoe was a very nice person who made Sofie relax and dare to be herself.

She realized that the real reason didn't matter. The important thing was that for the first time since school began, she was having fun with somebody – during school hours.

"Will you fish me out if I fall out of the canoe tomorrow?" Zoe had asked when they sat down at one of the round tables in the lunchroom.

"Sure," Sofie had said, somewhat tongue in cheek. "As long as it doesn't put me in any danger." Since the canoeing group was the only one with room for more people during the field day, Jimmy had ordered Zoe to join it. Sofie was very happy about this and was almost looking forward to tomorrow's adventure.

"Great!" Zoe loaded in a new mouthful of lasagna. "Mmm," she said with approval. "Is the food always this good?"

Sofie couldn't answer that question. She'd had lunch here every day, but had been so busy keeping track of Nathalie – and thinking about her worries – that she hadn't even noticed how the food tasted.

"Mostly," she said.

"Why don't we sit with the others?" Zoe asked after chewing lustfully for a while. She nodded at a table where most of the girls in the class were sitting. Including Nathalie.

Sofie hesitated. Should she tell the truth? What if Zoe thought that there was something wrong with *her* and joined the other girls instead?

But after considering this for a minute, Sofie decided to tell the entire story. From the first day up until now. Zoe seemed to be somebody who could think for herself. She

130

certainly could make her own judgments without giving in to anybody's pressure.

Sofie tried not to exaggerate her story.

"What a pain!" Zoe exclaimed when Sofie was done. She shook her head, dreads flying around her face. "What's wrong with her?"

"No idea." Sofie relaxed when Zoe seemed to root for her. "Lack of self-confidence, maybe?"

"Hm." Zoe's forehead wrinkled as she scraped the plate with her fork. "And those two girls who always follow her around, who are they?"

Sofie told her about Peter No-Tail and his stupid but loyal friends Bill and Bull. Zoe giggled.

"Imagine that; we have Barbie, Ken, Bill and Bull right here at school!" she said.

When they had carried their trays and were leaving the room, Zoe turned to Sofie.

"So what do you do when you're not in school?" she asked.

This was the next test. Suppose Zoe was one of those girls who hated horses? She certainly didn't look like a horse girl – but on the other hand, she didn't look like a minister girl either, Sofie thought, making it her turn to giggle.

"What's so funny?" Zoe raised her eyebrows.

"I'm sorry," Sofie quickly said. She hoped that she hadn't offended the black-clad girl. "I just thought about something funny. Well, actually… I'm into horses. You asked what I do in my spare time," she explained.

"You ride?" Zoe didn't look either happy or sad at this.

"I've only tried riding once." Sofie told her about her adventure on Saturday and about Humleby Farm. And while she was at it, she couldn't refrain from mentioning George's horses too.

131

"It sounds like you're pretty busy," Zoe commented.

"Yes." They had arrived at their lockers and Sofie opened hers to check her schedule, which she had carelessly thrown on top of the books. "A little *too* busy," she went on. "Mom and Dad are going to have the horses moved in a week, since I don't have the time for them. I'm just so sorry for George…"

Zoe opened her locker and peered at her behind the door.

"I wish I could help you, but I'm afraid I don't know too much about horses. But dogs, on the other hand!"

"You have a dog?" Sofie pulled her history book out and grabbed a pencil and an eraser.

Zoe, not having any books as yet, got out a pencil box.

"Two of them! And they're mine," she said proudly. "A golden retriever and a Bernese mountain dog. I've had them since they were puppies."

"What are their names?" Sofie asked. She had always wanted a pet but never had one. Elizabeth was scared of dogs and a cat wouldn't have worked out in the semi-detached house in London. Stefan hated rats, mice and all other rodents, which had made hamsters and guinea pigs impossible, too.

"Bella and Scooby." Zoe smiled. "Not very fancy names, but I was only eight when I got them."

"It would be fun to meet them sometimes," Sofie heard herself saying. She bit her tongue. Had she gone too far?

"That would be great! Where do you live?" Zoe didn't seem offended at all. She looked glad.

Sofie could feel happiness spreading throughout her body, and somewhere in the back of her head Jojo's words were echoing, "There has to be at least *one* girl in your class who isn't *totally* brain-dead."

132

The Power of One

"I think I made a friend," Sofie whispered with her nose in Speedy's golden blonde mane. "Aren't you a little happy for me?" The chestnut snorted and Sofie tenderly caressed his neck. "No?" she softly went on. "That's all right. I know it's hard to be happy for others when you're not feeling good yourself."

Sofie had walked straight to Humleby Farm when she got off the school bus on Monday afternoon. She was so happy that her insides bubbled, and it didn't seem like any fun to go home to an empty, quiet house.

Sofie inhaled the sweetish stable smell. For the first time in a long time, she felt the peace that used to come over her when she was in the stable. She loved the homey sounds. Hooves treading around in the sawdust or scraping a little against the cement floor underneath. Soft neighing. A thud when one of the big animals happened to come in contact with a wall or push against his or her feeder.

It was great to be in the stable without having to work, just this once.

Tina stood just inside the door, packing two big nylon bags. Rocky was racing at Solvalla tomorrow, which meant an early departure from Humleby. Sofie knew that Tina wanted to be well prepared to avoid having to hurry in the morning.

They seldom left the day before a race, even if the trip to Solvalla took almost seven hours. Tommy preferred having the horses resting at home for as long as possible.

"You seem in a better mood today!" Tina called from her corner. "Has anything happened?"

Sofie wondered how her happiness could show at that distance. They hadn't even said hi to each other yet.

She left Speedy for a while and walked over to the horse minder.

"A new girl came to our class today!" she said cheerily.

Tina, who was almost standing on her head in one of the bags, straightened and smiled.

"Oh?" She massaged the small of her back with one hand. "That's great! Does she seem all right?"

The question really was unnecessary. As soon as Sofie had walked into the passageway, Tina could tell that she was moving in a different way. Compared to last week, her back was straighter and there was more spring in her steps; she didn't drag herself along like a zombie.

"Yes." Sofie's eyes glittered. "Zoe doesn't look like somebody you make friends with, but she seems great. Nice, smart and fun."

"That's great!" Tina looked sincerely glad. "Now, of course, I want to hear all about how she looks…"

By the time Sofie had quoted almost every word that she and Zoe had said during the day, and painted a clear picture of the black-clad girl, Tina was done packing. The horse minder closed the bags, put the grooming box next to it and let the flat case with a newly oiled harness and racing bridle hang on the hook outside Rocky's box.

"I'm really happy for you!" she said, placing the bags

134

even closer to the wall. "And I seem to remember that I was sure everything would work out, even last week." She turned to Sofie and winked.

"Yes… I know you did." Sofie smiled a big smile. "But it isn't that easy to believe people who say 'it's going to be all right' when most of your life feels hopeless."

"I understand that," Tina said.

"There were so many problems then," Sofie went on, feeling a need to explain. "A new school, Nathalie, Speedy's knee and George's accident…"

"Yes, and speaking about that… How are 'your' mares?" Tina asked with curiosity. "I've heard about the food thief."

Sofie sighed and felt her heart sinking. Zoe had made her forget completely about Lisa and Mrs. Brown. Actually, she hadn't thought about George's horses even once all afternoon, and now she was suddenly reminded of them. She gave Tina a short, bleak rundown of the situation.

"The horses won't suffer from being moved to another stable for a while," Tina said when Sofie was done. "It might even be good for them."

"It's not the horses I'm worried about," Sofie admitted. "It's George. He's going to be so sad when he hears that they have to move. And it's going to be a much longer trip for him if he wants to go and see them. I don't think he'll be able to drive for some time – and to get to the other stable, you have to drive."

Tina nodded.

"I see what you mean. But doesn't he need a car to get out here, too?"

"Yes," Sofie said. "But somebody could pick him up at the bus stop a couple of times a week. It's not that far."

At that moment, Isabelle put her head in through the stable door.

135

"Hi! You're here, Sofie? I thought you'd be home, studying like a maniac." Isabelle grinned. "Wasn't that what you were going to do when you got rid of the evening chores with Lisa and Mrs. Brown?"

Sofie understood the taunt.

"I'm on my way," she said. "I just wanted to say hello to Speedy."

Isabelle laughed.

"You don't have to leave on account of me, I was just kidding." She turned to Tina. "So how's our favorite guy doing?"

"Well..." Tina smiled. "I guess about the same."

"No swelling or anything like that? On the knee, I mean?" Isabelle stepped into the passageway and leaned against Tornado's box.

"No, it looks fine," Tina assured her. "Speedy's fine. I guess he's a little irritated about having to rest, of course, but he seems to have accepted the situation."

Isabelle and Sofie walked together to Speedy's box.

"Horses are smart." Isabelle let Speedy smell her hand before she caressed his forehead. "They sort of seem to understand when they have to take it easy. That it's for their own good."

Sofie agreed. Speedy usually hated being in his box more than necessary, and he had been a little edgy right after the operation, but now he seemed at peace.

"You're a good boy, aren't you?" Sofie pulled her fingers through the horse's mane, thinking about George's horses. How could she stop them from being moved?

Was she lazy? Shouldn't she be able to take care of two horses a few hours every day?

But then she thought about everything that might happen to them. No, she really didn't want to carry all the

136

responsibility for Lisa and Mrs. Brown by herself. She really, really didn't want to do that.

From: Sofie Lindquist <sofiesofine@swede-mail.com>
Date: Monday, September 2, 2 2009, 17:32
To: Joanna Nilsson <jojo_sweetie@britmail.com>
Subject: Better

Hi, Jojo!

I actually should be studying, now that I finally have the time. But I can't concentrate – way too many thoughts are spinning around in my head.

There's a new girl in class! Her name is Sarah, but she calls herself Zoe, and I like her. And she seems to like me, too, so I hope, hope, hope we'll be friends.

Zoe is one of those girls that you and I would have wrinkled our noses at if we had seen her on the tube. I guess we would have called her a punk or something like that. Actually, it's possible that Zoe listens to punk, but I don't mind that as long as I don't have to listen myself.

I actually feel happy today – even if I'm not sure I should. Nothing has changed, really, except that I spoke to Zoe. Speedy is still newly operated on and stands sulking in his box. Nathalie is still mean and George's horses are on their way to be banished from the village. ("Thanks" to my parents.)

George's horses are my biggest problem right now. I promised *him I'd take care of Lisa and Mrs. Brown, and now he might not be able to see them for months!!! How can I ever tell him?*

But somehow, life feels easier now all the same. I think I would be able to deal with ten Nathalies as long as I have somebody like Zoe. My big fear is that Nathalie will "enlist" her and that I'll be alone again.

That thing about the power of one isn't true, whatever people say.

Did I tell you about Adam, by the way? I think I forgot that, but I have to tell you another day because now I HAVE to do my homework.

Hugs, Sofie

From: Joanna Nilsson <jojo_sweetie@britmail.com>
Date: Monday, September 2, 2009, 18:30
To: Sofie Lindquist <sofiesofine@swede-mail.com>
Subject: Re: Better

Sofie, I might strangle you!

Don't you know it's absolutely prohibited to mention a guy without writing anything more? How long will I have to wait for more information?

Jojo

P.S. Tell Zoe she can only borrow you for a while. You and I are best friends. (Or were, at least, before you sent that latest e-mail. WHO is Adam???)

The Catcher in the Rye?

Sofie's heart suddenly jumped when she saw Adam in the middle of the crowd, waiting for the bus in the schoolyard. So, he was going canoeing, too!

She stood at a proper distance from Adam and his friend, but still close enough to see them clearly. Adam really was cute. His blond locks looked almost golden in the September sun.

"Who are you staring at?" Zoe nudged at her.

"Um… Nobody," Sofie answered, feeling herself blushing.

"I don't believe you."

Zoe was dressed in black sweatpants and a black hooded sweater. Her white dreadlocks were held together with a pink ribbon. A black backpack hung over one shoulder.

"It's a good thing it isn't raining," Sofie said to change the subject.

Zoe nodded.

"Yeah, we won't get wet for that reason anyway." She smiled a crooked smile. "Have you been in a canoe before?"

"Once or twice. You?"

"Never."

139

Sofie was beginning to understand why Zoe was talking so much about water and falling into the lake.

"It's not that hard to paddle a canoe," Sofie said, feeling a little satisfied that for once *she* wasn't the one worrying. "And we'll be paddling in a lake. There won't be any currents. And no big waves."

"All right." Zoe didn't look very comfortable.

Just then, the bus turned into the schoolyard. Jimmy, dressed in bright green tight sweatpants and an equally green sleeveless top, came jogging out of the school.

"The bus is here!" he called out. "Stand in line!"

The students started walking toward the bus. Zoe leaned her head against Sofie and whispered in her ear, "Help! Ken has turned into a frog! What are we going to do?"

"Kiss him! He might actually be a prince!"

Both girls started giggling helplessly.

"It's nice to see I'm not the only one who thinks it's going to be fun to go canoeing," Jimmy said with a smile as the girls, giggling violently, got on the bus.

Sofie tried to smile back at him, but guessed that it looked more like some kind of funny face.

She was still giggling when she thudded down next to Zoe in the back of the bus moments later. After a minute, she had enough control over her breath to speak.

"Wow! It's been a long time since I laughed like that." She hardly dared to look at Zoe, worrying that she might break down in giggles again.

At that moment, a head of blond, curly hair appeared right in front of her eyes.

Sofie swallowed. Adam was sitting in the seat in front of her!

Zoe gave Sofie an amused look.

"So you were looking at 'nobody' before?" she whispered.

140

Sofie hated that everybody could read her like an open book, but she was firmly resolved that Zoe wouldn't learn anything about her feelings for Adam. Not yet. She wasn't even sure about her own feelings. And she had only known Zoe for one day.

"So, did you feed those horses this morning?" Zoe asked after a while. The teasing spark had gone from her eyes, and she seemed to have given up trying to worm any of Sofie's secrets out of her.

"Yep. At five thirty, I was in the stable, pouring oats into two buckets."

"Five thirty!" Zoe stared at Sofie. "For real?"

"Why would I lie about it?" Sofie smiled. "It's actually pretty nice to get up early." She wondered if she had said that last bit to impress Adam. "Well, once you're out of bed, anyway," she added.

"I think it sounds awful!" Zoe exclaimed.

"You get used to it…" Sofie sighed. "George called last night again, well, the owner of the horses, you know. And I couldn't tell him that his horses will have to move this time either! He seemed a little better and talked about coming out to see them soon. He said he missed them!"

"You have to tell him the truth before he's standing there in front of an empty paddock." Zoe looked a little troubled. "Haven't your parents talked to him?"

"I want to tell him myself. I'm the one who promised to take care of Lisa and Mrs. Brown… But it's harder than I thought. And I guess I've been thinking all along that it's going to work out somehow."

Zoe shrugged.

"They won't be going away forever!" she said. "How bad can it be?"

"I'd go crazy if somebody suddenly moved Speedy."

"Speedy?"

Sofie told her about her chestnut favorite. When she was done, after about ten minutes, Zoe said, "Sounds like a fairytale horse. Is he for real?"

❀ ❀ ❀ ❀

"Help!" Zoe whined, standing wobbling in the yellow canoe.

She looked so funny that Sofie had to laugh out loud.

"Sit down!" she said. "You can't stand there like a flagpole."

Zoe cautiously sat on the front seat. She turned her head and looked pleadingly at Sofie.

"Don't laugh at me." She lowered her voice. "I-I'm afraid of water."

Afraid of water? Sofie almost giggled again, but when she saw Zoe's pale face she realized that the otherwise so cool girl was actually serious.

"But you can swim, can't you?" Sofie almost got a little worried. She didn't know if she was a great lifeguard. She had never tried with a living person, only a doll. And that was when she learned to swim, six or seven years ago.

"Well, sort of…" Zoe smiled thinly.

Sofie was thankful that everybody was wearing a life-vest.

"I *can* swim," Zoe explained. "In a pool, where I can reach the bottom. But I panic when the water's deep. And black…" She looked with disgust at the water, which seemed almost brown-black on the muddy bottom.

"Well then!" Sofie tried to encourage her new friend. "You won't fall in if we take it easy. I'll be sitting here in back, so I'll do the steering. You just have to paddle."

"All right…"

They were told to paddle around the little lake in a line.

142

Jimmy and another phys. ed. teacher would paddle in front and lead the way, while two other teachers would be in another canoe, bringing up the rear.

To Sofie's great joy, Adam and his friend had happened to fall in right behind Sofie and Zoe. Sofie hoped to catch a few things that the boys might talk about during the canoeing. The only thing that bothered her a little was that they would be able to study her paddling technique the whole time.

Jimmy had lectured them on how to steer their canoes in the best way, and now he gestured to the first canoe in the line.

"Let's go!" he called. "Now remember, no tomfoolery! Everybody is to sit down, and if you run into any problems, just call out to us."

One by one, the canoes floated out onto the lake. They had been ordered to keep a certain distance between each other, to avoid collisions.

Zoe looked terrified, and Sofie tried to calm her down.

"It's going to work out fine!" she cheerily said. "Just paddle on."

Zoe answered her with a tormented smile.

And it did work out fine. After a couple of hundred yards, Zoe started relaxing and the girls found an even rhythm. They were about five yards behind the canoe in front of them and the group had been ordered to stay close to the shore.

Sofie actually enjoyed sitting there. Everybody except for the girls in the first canoe was silent, concentrating on the task at hand. This made it possible to hear the rhythmic splashing of paddles hitting the water, mixed with the jabber from ducks and other seabirds that were occasionally visible in the reeds. A flock of geese flew south above the lake. There was no doubt that autumn was coming.

Every once in a while the students had to duck for branches reaching out over the glittering water. Sofie found it all beautiful. Not just nice, but beautiful. She couldn't remember the last time she was out in nature for nature's own sake, without being on her way to or from a stable.

Zoe also seemed lost in her thoughts – or maybe struck dumb with fear – and they didn't say anything to each other for quite a long time.

All the time, Sofie was aware of Adam's presence behind her, but this mostly felt good. They were doing all right, after all.

"Can we change sides?" Sofie asked after a while. "My arm is starting to hurt."

Zoe turned around.

"Okay." She lifted her paddle across the bow, suddenly fumbled and – dropped it!

"Nooo!" she screamed, hanging out over the side of the canoe to catch it.

The canoe began to lean over to the right and Sofie tried to stop it by throwing herself to the left. The only problem was that Zoe happened to get hold of her paddle at that moment and suddenly stood up.

Which meant that their canoe leaned too far to the left.

"What's happening?" Zoe screamed in a panic.

She dropped her paddle again. And in the next moment, both of them were splashing around in the cold water.

"Heeelp!" Zoe moaned. "Heeelp!"

Sofie swam over to her.

"Take it easy," she said. "You're floating thanks to your lifejacket, so don't worry!"

Zoe's eyes were wide with fear.

"B-but the water's so… Leeches! I bet this whole lake is full of leeches!"

"You're wearing clothes," Sofie said reasonably. "Help me turn the canoe over instead." She looked around. "And we have to get hold of the paddles, too."

Zoe kept splashing around wildly. She was probably trying to scare the imaginary leeches away.

"So, you need some help, or what?" The voice came from above.

Sofie raised her head and looked into a couple of lovely brown-green eyes. Adam's eyes. He leaned out of his canoe, looking at her with amusement.

Sofie almost said, "Yes! Please! Save me!"

But of course, she didn't.

"Would you help me turn the canoe over?" she asked instead. "My friend isn't too much help right now…" She threw a glance at Zoe, who was still floating like a cork but persisted in flailing her arms and legs.

"I don't know how much I can help while I'm in the canoe," Adam said. "But we can always try."

A thousand thoughts were whirling around in Sofie's head. How would they get up in the canoe again? Why did she have to look like a drowning rat the first time Adam spoke to her? What would they do about Zoe? Would Jimmy be angry?

Adam and his friend made a few fumbling attempts at turning the canoe over. They didn't do very well. But by the time the two teachers who were last in the line had made it to the scene of the accident, Sofie had at least managed to get hold of both paddles.

"Are you okay?" one of the teachers asked.

She nodded.

"Yes, but Zoe is scared of leeches, and we can't turn the canoe over."

"I guess you'll have to push it to the shore," the Swedish teacher said, not seeming very worried about Zoe's state. "You think you can make it?"

Sofie nodded again. Zoe still looked scared to death but seemed to at least hear what was said. She nodded.

"Do you have extra clothes in the cabin?"

"At least I do," Sofie said, and Zoe nodded speechlessly. She was still thrashing around, but not that wildly now.

"Good."

The entire group had stopped and turned their canoes to see the upside down canoe and the two girls in the water. Scattered giggles could be heard across the water.

Strangely enough, Sofie didn't find the situation especially embarrassing. It felt like she had experienced far worse things lately. And she had a feeling that she and Zoe would be able to laugh about this in a while – when Zoe was over the shock.

Well, it actually was a little embarrassing, but that was just because Adam was there.

Jimmy and his colleague had turned back and paddled past the students in front of the overturned canoe.

"Oh my!" he said, smiling at Sofie. He didn't seem angry, only a bit troubled. "Are you okay?"

"Yes, I think." She smiled back. "But it's a little cold."

Jimmy turned to Zoe.

"You'll just tire yourself out if you thrash around like that," he said. "Save your energy for towing the canoe instead."

After a short conference it was decided that the Swedish teacher and his colleague would follow the girls to the cabin where they had rented the canoes, so that Sofie and

Zoe could change clothes. The girls would pull their canoe up on the shore right there and get it later. Jimmy and the other students would go on as planned.

When the girls finally stood on the shore, water dripping heavily from clothes and hair, Zoe exclaimed, "They were no great heroes, those two guys behind us."

"What?" Sofie hadn't even thought that Zoe had noticed them.

"I really tried to get their attention with some theatrics, but they didn't seem to care. Suppose I had been scared for real!"

Sofie smiled.

"You *were* scared for real."

Zoe was silent for a moment, looking out across the water. Then she said, "Yeah, all right. I was."

Real Rescue

"Aren't you going swimming again?"

"Was the water nice?"

All the students seemed to have "funny" comments when they returned to the canoe rental to have lunch.

Sofie and Zoe were sitting on a wooden bench outside the rental. They leaned against the cabin wall and let the mild sun warm them as they ate the sandwiches they had brought and drank hot chocolate.

"The water was wonderful!" Zoe said to a big guy in ninth grade. "Just try it yourself! You want me to help throw you in?"

Sofie giggled and shut her eyes. It felt good to sit on a bench in the sun together with Zoe, far away from Nathalie. If she just didn't have to call George this afternoon things would be even better. Her conscience nagged at her as soon as she thought about Lisa and Mrs. Brown.

Suddenly someone sat down next to her. And even before she turned, she could somehow feel those eyes.

"Hi!" Adam said. The bench creaked precariously. "Is there room for me, too?"

Sofie's heart started pounding wildly in her chest.

"Don't think so," Zoe said immediately. "Not after

148

that worthless rescue attempt out on the lake." She smiled impishly.

Adam grinned.

"Well, it's not that easy to save somebody who's flailing her arms like a windmill. And you seemed to be able to save yourselves pretty well."

"It wasn't such a big deal," Sofie chimed in, feeling that she had to say something.

They sat in silence for a while. Zoe slurped noisily every time she sipped her chocolate. The wind whispered softly in the trees behind the cabin, and far away they could hear the noise of fifteen kids let loose in the country.

Sofie grew more and more nervous with every passing second. Why couldn't she think about anything sensible to say?

"But…" Adam quickly cleared his throat. "I… um… I understand that you have other problems…"

Sofie drew a breath. What did he mean? Was he going to defend Nathalie now? Had Nathalie asked Adam to tell Sofie off?

"W-what do you mean?"

Adam's face went beet red.

"Well, you know… On the bus here… Well, I couldn't help hearing you talk about those horses…"

Sofie let out her breath. So Nathalie had nothing to do with this.

"What horses?" she said stupidly, thinking she heard Zoe stifle a giggle.

"Well…" Adam seemed almost irritated at having to explain. "You were talking about two horses that have to be moved. Because somebody's in the hospital. And because you don't have the time to take care of them yourself."

Sofie looked at the curly-haired boy with suspicion. Was

149

he going to make fun of her for her not being able to take care of Lisa and Mrs. Brown?

"And?" She looked at him.

Adam fidgeted a little and the bench creaked precariously again.

"Oh… I thought that maybe I could help out…"

Sofie rose to her feet and stared at him.

"For real?"

"Sure. Dad doesn't have that many horses right now… And his staff has to have something to do." Adam looked a little embarrassed. He wasn't used to girls staring at him in this way.

Sofie didn't know what to think. Should she actually dare to believe that Adam was telling the truth? Why would a guy in ninth grade, who seemed so popular, want to help a girl in seventh grade who had just moved to town?

"I can't pay you," she said.

"I wasn't counting on that."

"And you have to get up really early." Sofie gave him a searching look.

Adam smiled.

"Maybe you don't *want* any help?"

"Oh yes, yes!" Sofie said quickly. "I just can't understand that… that it's for real! You actually mean that you're ready to help me with two horses that you've never met – without being paid?"

"Aren't we talking about those two mares at the crossroads? Across from the white stable?"

"Yes…" Sofie looked at Adam with surprise.

"But that's perfect!" Zoe exclaimed, after having been unusually silent for a couple of minutes. "That means that Lisa and Mrs. Brown can stay and George can come and see them to his heart's content!"

151

Sofie looked down, trying to digest what she had just heard. She still couldn't really believe that Adam had offered to help her. Why in the world did he want to do that? He who, according to Nathalie, lived in a mansion and had a dad who worked with some of the best trotters in Sweden. Why did Adam want to help her with two nice, but average, trotters being trained by an amateur?

She could feel his worried looks. And Zoe's understanding ones.

So what was she waiting for?

Sofie looked straight into Adam's brown-green eyes and smiled.

"Thanks a lot!" she said. "I'd be very happy if you'd help me with George's horses."

Thanks!

Thanks to Hans and Mai Adielsson for letting me irregularly pester your staff. And lots of thanks to all horse-minders in Kvarnby for sharing your knowledge and experience.

An especially big thank you to Kit for invaluable help and many nice chats in the stable.

I also want to thank Happy Dancer and his buddies for inspiration and friendly receptions.

Last but not least: Thank you, Tore! (You'll know why when you read the book.) Neigh!

Malin Stehn